AF539808

Winds for Change

Dr. Nilakshi Choudhury, an accomplished author and humanitarian hailing from Barpeta Road, Assam, embodies the values instilled during her academic years at Barpeta Road and Guwahati Commerce College. Her pursuit of higher education in Delhi, specializing in Company Secretaryship, an MBA, and an LLB, laid the foundation for a remarkable journey. Since 2001, Dr. Choudhury has made significant contributions to the legal field, with roles in reputable firms like Fox Mandal Little N Associates and Vaish Associates Advocates. Her commitment to societal welfare is evident through advocacy seminars conducted across 12 states on Corporate Social Responsibility and Business Responsibility.

Apart from her legal practice at the Supreme Court of India since 2012, Dr. Choudhury, has played a pivotal role in philanthropic efforts with the central government scheme's for vocational training under the DDUGKY scheme, trained over 3000 underprivileged candidates across 5 states and facilitating placements in prestigious institutions and companies. In a spirit of humility, Dr. Choudhury founded "24x7nyaya" with a mission to provide legal assistance plans. This platform, boasting 1800+ lawyers across 12 countries, pioneers legal support for individuals, corporations, hospitals, and educational institutes at a nominal rate, resembling legal insurance. Notably, Dr. Choudhury is a member of the American Bar Association, the International Bar Association, and is qualified as an international arbitrator.

The global impact extends to the customization of a legal assistance plan for the Law Ministry of Sri Lanka. To date, 24x7nyaya has discreetly served over 70,000 people, with 600+ subscribers benefiting from comprehensive legal support. Dr. Nilakshi Choudhury has also served as a consultant to several embassies within the jurisdiction of India, providing professional advisory services in accordance with applicable laws and regulations.

This note humbly encapsulates the multifaceted journey of Dr. Nilakshi Choudhury, reflecting her unwavering dedication to law and society through diverse and unassuming accomplishments.

Winds for Change

Propelling Change in the Indian Judiciary

Dr. Nilakshi Choudhury

Published by
PRABHAT PRAKASHAN PVT. LTD.
4/19 Asaf Ali Road,
New Delhi-110 002 (INDIA)
e-mail: prabhatbooks@gmail.com

ISBN 978-93-5562-452-9
WINDS FOR CHANGE
by Dr. Nilakshi Choudhury

Edition
First, 2024

Price
₹ 500.00 (Rupees Five Hundred only)
$20 (US Dollar Twenty only)

Printed at
R-Tech Offset Printers, Delhi

This humble book is dedicated
to the cherished memory of my beloved father,
Shri Bidyananda Choudhury
who departed for the heavenly abode on the
16th of November 2019.

In the footsteps of my father, I find inspiration to share a tale that resonates with the pursuit of justice and the enduring spirit of selflessness. His legacy as an unsung hero, a compassionate soul dedicated to serving society, remains etched in my heart.

JUSTICE K.G. BALAKRISHNAN
Former Chief Justice of India
Former Chairperson National Human Rights Commission

Bungalow No.7, New Moti Bagh, New Delhi-110021
Email: officejusticekghalakrishnan@gmail.com
Mobile: +919717266700

To Whomsoever it may Concern

I would like to congratulate the author Dr. Nilakshi Choudhury on her seminal work "Winds for Change in the Indian Judiciary", a book that delves into pivotal changes that time requires the legal field to go through.

I have been at the helm of the Judiciary in Bharat and can say without a doubt that such thinkers like the esteemed author are required to bring about positive change in the system and its ancillaries

Despite hurdles and challenges the author has been able to produce an interesting read and a detailed body of information emanating from her own life experience.

I wish Dr. Nilakshi Choudhury all the best for her book and her future endeavors, may she contribute more to the legal field in Bharat for many more years to come.

Wishing all the best.

(JUSTICE K.G. BALAKRISHNAN)

New Delhi
12.02.2024

Dr. WIJEYADASA RAJAPAKSHE
President's Counsel
Ph.D. University of Colombo
Ph.D. University of Kelaniya
LL.D. (Honoris Causa) Commonwealth University

Dr. Nilakshi Choudhury, FCS, LLB, MBA Finance, a versatile legal consultant and an exuberant writer has undertaken a onerous task of revitalizing the social fabric of India through innovative legal thinking and restorative righteous principles and values which had been treasured for few millennia. Being one of the oldest civilization, India has played a most pivotal role in exploring and inculcating oriental ethos and universal virtue enhancing the standard of the humanity. The deep-rooted moral principles which were evolved blending with legal norms has reached to high standard which is remarkable in the domain of the world's largest democracy. But it does not mean that it is without the needs of more reforms. Dr. Nilakshi Choudhury, with her vast reservoir of knowledge and experience in diversified fields has thought fit to expand the existing legal framework towards a new dimension by traversing through novel ideas befitting to the society she lives in.

Principles of democracy in the modern world go across the borders with the quests of better life standards and well-being of the society. She has endeavored to find ways and means to strike a balance between the power on the one side of the scale and the accountability on the other side of it, in the rapidly changing world. Corruption free governance is a dream of every citizen in a democratic country and the rulers are bound to uphold the rule of law even though the heaven falls as it is an indispensable tool of the State. The Author in her wisdom has delved upon many complex disciplines such as human rights, public safety, animal welfare, effectiveness of corporate governance and corporate responsibility, delay of the administration of justice, legal reforms for sex workers etc., in an orderly array.

There is an unimpeachable trend in democracies that the rulers are only the custodians of the people who have delegated their sovereignty temporarily to exercise for the safety and the well-being of the people at large. Taking into consideration of the responsibility of the rulers to protect and preserve the environment not only for the present generation but also for the future generation Justice Weeramanthry, (a Sri Lankan who presided the bench) in the International Court of Justice in the case of Gabčíkovo-Nagymaros Project (Hungary/Slovakia) has held that the "imperative of balancing the needs of the present generation with those of posterity is imperative in State governance." It demonstrates the true meaning of the justice which denotes unequivocally that the rulers are only the custodians and they are obligated to wield their powers for the betterment of the present as well as of the future

In that context, I commend the intellectual exercise displayed by the writer and I wish that she may add many more writings towards the enhancement of the quality of legal literature, not only in India but also universally.

Wijayadasa Rajapakshe

(Dr. Wijayadasa Rajapakshe)
President's Counsel
Minister of Justice, Prison Affairs and Constitutional Reforms of the Republic of Sri Lanka
On this 10th day February 2024

الإمـــارات للـمحـامـاة

EMIRATES ADVOCATES

P.O. Box 9055, Dubai, U.A.E.

Tel: (971) 43304343, Fax: (971) 43303993

E-mail: contact@emiratesadvocates.com

www.emiratesadvocates.com

Dear Readers,

It is with great pleasure that I unveil the insightful work penned by Dr. Nilakshi Choudhury—"Winds for Change: Navigating Legal Reforms in India."

In this comprehensive exploration, Dr. Choudhury delves into the dynamic landscape of legal reforms in India, offering a profound understanding of the winds of change sweeping through our legal system. Her meticulous research and keen insights make this book an invaluable resource for anyone seeking to comprehend the intricate tapestry of legal evolution in our nation.

As we embark on this intellectual journey, I am confident that "Winds for Change" will serve as a guiding beacon, enlightening readers about the transformative currents shaping the legal domain.

Congratulations to Dr. Nilakshi Choudhury on this remarkable contribution.

Best Regards,

Dr. Khalid Almheiri

Chairman, Emirates Advocates

Chief Advisor to The King

VIMLESH KUMAR SHUKLA
Former Judge
High Court of Allahabad

37, High Court Judges Colony
Sector-105, Noida-20130

Date: 10.02.2024

To

Dr. Nilakshi Choudhury

"Know yourself to know the world."

"Winds for Change in the Indian Judiciary" is a book, which clearly fits in the said context.

It's a privilege to go through the forth coming book described above. As the name suggests, 'Change' is the hallmark in context of Indian Judiciary which has evolved itself over a period of time, Our Constitution is called a living document, as Constitution accepts the necessity of modifications according to changing needs of the society and in actual working of Constitution there has been enough flexibility by way of purposive interpretations.

The Author, has fully succeeded in her pursuit and has shed much more than the required light on the pressing issues and the opportunity Indian Judiciary had and will have in future. The book makes an interesting reading and she has attempted to address all relevant issues, that is bound to appeal to all the readers.

I congratulate her for sharing her wisdom and experiences with people, either connected with law or un-connected with law. Wishing her the 'Best of Wishes.'

V.K. Shukla

(V.K. SHUKLA)

Dr. Bhaskar Chatterjee I.A.S. (Retd.)
Former Secretary Govt. of India,
Former Director General,
Indian Institute of Corporate Affairs
Ministry of Corporate Affairs

To Whomsoever it May Concern

The Indian judiciary is an indispensable institution in the country's democratic framework. Its role as the guardian of the Constitution, protector of rights, and dispenser of justice is essential for upholding the principles of integrity, equality, and democracy. By upholding the rule of law and promoting good governance, the judiciary plays a crucial role in ensuring that India remains a vibrant and democratic society.

As a former bureaucrat, having served the nation for a little over 41 years, I have always viewed our judiciary as one of the finest in the world. It has been faced with multitudes of challenges and has been buffeted by many storms and controversies. Amidst it all, it has remained a bulwark, steadfast in its values and determined in its purpose of providing "Justice for All." I have had occasion to sit as magistrate in my earlier years in the bureaucracy and have thereafter, sought judicial intervention during many occasions in my long bureaucratic career.

It is, therefore, a matter of great pride that we have a major contribution to the evolution of our judicial system from a practitioner, a researcher and social reformer of the stature of Nilakshi Choudhury. She has addressed– in her book entitled *Nyaya-Winds: Propelling Change in the Indian Judiciary*– issues of contemporary importance in many aspects of our lives which impact and challenge the judicial mind. She has dealt with issues such as a nation's battle with crime and delayed justice, redefining the paradigm of reservation, strengthening mandatory provisions under Companies Act, the battle against corruption and corrupt practice etc. with great courage and conviction.

I earnestly believe that this thought provoking and stimulating work written in an informative yet very readable style deserves to be perused, not only by lawyers and judges but by all stakeholders who have an interest in our judicial system or have had any interaction with our courts.

No system, however steadfast, or solid remains static or is beyond improvement. In determining the course of the evolution of our national judicial system, I believe that this book has a significant role to play. It provides many pointers, perspectives and insights that every reader will appreciate and value.

I wish the book and its author all the very best on this epic occasion!

Disclaimer

The views and opinions expressed in this book on "Winds for Change in the Indian Judiciary" are solely those of the author, based on her personal experiences and observations over the years. The intention behind this work is to initiate a constructive dialogue and reflection on potential improvements within the Indian judicial system.

It is important to note that the author's perspective is offered with the utmost respect for all individuals, their sentiments, and the broader societal context. The purpose of this book is not to offend or hurt the feelings or egos of any person or group. Instead, it aims to contribute to an informed discussion about possible transformations that could lead to a safer and more just society.

The author acknowledges that the issues surrounding the Indian judiciary are complex and multifaceted, and any proposed solutions are presented with humility and a genuine desire for the betterment of humanity. The goal is to explore avenues for positive change that can ultimately benefit mankind and foster a society with reduced crime and increased harmony.

Readers are encouraged to approach the content with an open mind and engage in thoughtful discourse. The author invites readers to consider the ideas presented, challenge them, and contribute to a collective effort toward a more equitable and effective judicial system.

In no way does this book claim to possess all the answers, but rather it seeks to encourage meaningful conversations and promote a spirit of collaboration in pursuit of a brighter future for Indian society.

—Dr. Nilakshi Choudhury

Preface

It is with immense pleasure and gratitude that I present "Nyaya-Winds: Propelling Change in the Indian Judiciary." This book represents the culmination of years of research, dedication, and collaboration, and I am deeply grateful to all those who have played a significant role in bringing this project to fruition.

First and foremost, I extend my heartfelt thanks to my friend and mentor, Pradeep Baba Madhok, whose unwavering support and guidance have been instrumental in shaping my thoughts and ideas. Your wisdom and encouragement have been a constant source of inspiration throughout this journey.

Arijit, my consort your role as a critic and a pillar of support has been invaluable in shaping my endeavours, both personal and professional. My dear daughter, Rudrani, your resilience, and maturity are a constant inspiration. Watching you grow and navigate life with grace and determination fills my heart with pride.

I am thankful to my team, Abhishek & Deepika, for their valuable support in bringing this book to life.

In "Nyaya-Winds," my aim is to shed light on the pressing issues and opportunities within the Indian judiciary. I have endeavoured to offer a comprehensive analysis of the challenges that our legal system faces while also proposing viable solutions that can steer us towards a brighter future.

This book delves into the transformation of the Indian judiciary, emphasizing the need for transparency, efficiency, and empathy in the pursuit of justice. Through each chapter, I have sought to explore topics that hold significant importance in our society, urging for a thoughtful reflection on the path we choose to embark upon.

In the pages that follow, readers will encounter a vision of a technologically advanced judiciary that is rooted in the principles of fairness and accessibility. I believe that harnessing the potential of technology can revolutionize the way justice is delivered and received.

I must acknowledge that no work is without its limitations, and I recognize that this book may not encompass every aspect of the vast landscape of the Indian judiciary. However, my hope is that "Nyaya-Winds" will spark thoughtful conversations, inspire further research, and contribute to the ongoing discourse on judicial reform.

Lastly, I express my gratitude to all the readers who embark on this intellectual journey with me. Your interest in this subject and willingness to engage with the ideas presented here make this endeavour more meaningful.

Thank you for joining me on this quest to propel change in the Indian judiciary. Together, let us navigate the winds of justice, towards a more equitable and enlightened society.

—Dr. Nilakshi Choudhury

List of Abbreviations used

A.I.R. – All India Reporters
A.L.S. – Amyotrophic Lateral Sclerosis
app. – Appendix
art. – Article
Bom. – Bombay
B.C. – Before Christ
Ch. – Chapter
Cr.LJ – Criminal Law Journal
Cl. – Clause
Col. – Column
Const. – Constitution of India
e.g. – For example
Engl – England
etc. – etcetera
expln. – Explanation
Guj – Gujarat
HCC – High Court Cases
hdg. – Heading
Ibid. – Of Ibidem (in the Same page)
I.C. – Indian Cases
ISBN – International Standard Book Number
i.e. – That is
I.P.C. – Indian Penal Code
ISP. – Internet Service Provider

No. – Number
PAS – Physician Assisted Suicide
PVS – Permanent Vegetative State
PAD - Physician aid – in -dying
PARA – Paragraph
S – Section
S.C. – Supreme Court
SS – Sections
SCC. – Supreme Court Cases
SCR – Supreme Court Report

Contents

Nyaya-Winds: Propelling Change in the Indian Judiciary

Introduction:

"Nyaya," we unravel a poignant account of a man who walked the path of righteousness, embodying the virtues of honesty and benevolence. It reflects a society where respect and veneration are bestowed upon individuals for their contributions, much like the revered idols of India, such as Hey Ram and Hey Krishna. In this narrative, we delve into the life of Sri Bidyananda Choudhury, affectionately known as Hey Bidyananda, whose noble deeds left an indelible mark on the town of 'Barpeta Road.'

A Philanthropist's Tale:

Sri Bidyananda Choudhury, the visionary architect of 'Barpeta Road,' sculpted the town's destiny, transforming it into the thriving commercial hub of Assam. Yet, his altruistic endeavours went unnoticed, and his magnanimity was taken for granted. He erected the grandest shopping complex, selflessly granting humble shopkeepers a chance to realize their dreams by offering them spaces at nominal rents. The rent increase of 4% every five years was a gesture of both kindness and foresight.

Betrayal and Justice Delayed:

As the years passed, Shri Bidyananda Choudhury's health waned, and he contemplated retiring to a metro city for better healthcare. In an act of goodwill, he extended a year-long opportunity to the shopkeepers to purchase or lease the premises they occupied. However, this noble intention was twisted against him, leading to a lawsuit that affected his mind, body, and soul. The wheels of justice turned slowly in the lower courts, exacerbating his plight until his unfortunate demise.

The Soul's Quest for Peace:

Witnessing my father's devoted life and the tragic circumstances of his death left an indelible impact on my heart. Amidst the homage and processions that followed his passing, the haunting question remained - would the tribute offered in retrospect alleviate the suffering caused by delayed justice? The pursuit of truth, justice, and the quest for redemption echoes through the pages of this book.

A Call for Change:

In "Nyaya," we beckon for a transformation in the fabric of justice. We seek a world where noble souls like Sri Bidyananda Choudhury are honoured and protected, where justice is swift, and where the spirit of selflessness thrives. As we share this tale of resilience, empathy, and the pursuit of truth, we kindle the winds of change, urging the collective conscience of society to reflect upon the meaning of justice and the responsibilities we bear towards each other.

Conclusion:

"Nyaya: Winds of Change in the Indian Judiciary" offers

a poignant journey through a life marked by benevolence, betrayal, and the quest for justice. It is a tale that echoes the virtues of selfless service and compassion, reminding us that every action has consequences, and justice delayed can wound even the noblest of souls. In honouring the legacy of Sri Bidyananda Choudhury, may we find the courage to stand for justice and uphold the values that define the true essence of humanity.

Introduction:

The Indian judiciary is the cornerstone of our democratic system, upholding the principles of justice, equality, and fairness. Over the years, it has played a crucial role in safeguarding the rights and liberties of citizens. However, like any institution, it faces challenges and opportunities for improvement. "Nyaya-Winds" aims to explore the winds of change needed to enhance the efficiency, accessibility, and transparency of the Indian judiciary.

Reimagining Judicial Processes in small states:

Reimagining judicial processes involves modernizing and digitizing the legal system to make it more efficient, accessible, and resilient. While digitization can significantly improve the judicial process by reducing paperwork, enhancing communication, and streamlining procedures, it is essential to address the challenges and limitations posed by external factors such as the COVID-19 pandemic or administrative issues.

The situation in Assam highlights some of the real-world challenges that can hinder the implementation of a fully digitalized judicial process. These challenges include:

Lack of infrastructure and internet connectivity: In many regions, especially rural areas, the lack of proper infrastructure and internet connectivity can impede the smooth functioning of digital systems. This has led to delays in hearings and other legal processes.

Human resource constraints: Absence due to maternity leave or other reasons has disrupted the regular functioning of the court. There might be a need to establish systems for managing staff shortages effectively.

Administrative changes: Frequent changes in personnel and administrative roles have created disruptions and learning curves for new staff, impacting the efficiency of the court.

Technological literacy: The successful adoption of digitization in the legal system relies on ensuring that all stakeholders, including judges, lawyers, court staff, and litigants, are technologically literate and comfortable with using digital tools.

Ensuring access to justice: While digitization can offer benefits, it should not exclude individuals who may not have access to digital resources. Alternative solutions should be in place to accommodate all litigants.

To address these challenges and make the judicial process more robust, reimagining should focus on:

Hybrid approaches: Implementing a combination of in-person and online hearings to ensure continuity during emergencies while preserving the importance of physical hearings for some cases.

Investing in infrastructure and training: Governments should invest in improving infrastructure and provide training to all stakeholders to enhance their digital literacy and adaptability.

Backup and contingency plans: Develop robust backup plans to handle situations when key personnel are unavailable, ensuring minimal disruption to court proceedings.

Establishing e-filing and document management systems: Implement efficient e-filing and document management systems to reduce paperwork and streamline case management.

Encouraging ADR mechanisms: Promote Alternative Dispute Resolution (ADR) methods, such as mediation and arbitration, that can be conducted online and are often faster and more cost-effective.

Public awareness campaigns: Create awareness among the public about the digitized processes, available resources, and how to access them.

□

Chapter I

Enhancing Corporate Law for minimised litigation and maximized Compliance

Title: Amending Corporate Law to Restrict Conversion to Criminal or Civil Litigation

Introduction:

Corporate law plays a critical role in governing the operations and behaviour of businesses. One area of concern is the potential misuse of corporate structures to shield individuals from personal liability for criminal or civil actions. This chapter explores the need for amending corporate law to restrict such conversions, highlights examples of companies that have faced severe consequences, and emphasizes the importance of a corporate legal audit to minimize litigation risk. Introduction: In the ever-evolving business landscape, corporate law must adapt to address emerging challenges and promote a fair and efficient legal framework. This chapter delves into the pressing need for amending corporate law to minimize litigation and ensure maximum compliance. By exploring the limitations of existing regulations and identifying areas prone to legal disputes, this chapter advocates for proactive changes that foster corporate responsibility and mitigate the risk of litigation.

Limitations of Existing Regulations a. Ambiguities in the Law: Vague or unclear provisions in corporate law can lead to multiple interpretations, leaving room for legal disputes and inconsistent judgments.

Complexity and Burden: Overly complex regulations can burden businesses, increasing the likelihood of unintentional non-compliance and triggering litigation.

Enforcement Challenges: Weak enforcement mechanisms may enable unscrupulous actors to exploit loopholes, undermining the effectiveness of corporate regulations.

Addressing Emerging Challenges:

(a) Incorporating Technological Advancements: Amending corporate law to accommodate technological advancements can help regulate emerging business models and digital transactions, reducing the potential for disputes arising from legal uncertainty.

(b) Data Privacy and Security: Strengthening data protection regulations can safeguard businesses and consumers, minimizing litigation risks related to data breaches and cyberattacks.

Promoting Corporate Compliance:

(a) Emphasizing Corporate Social Responsibility (CSR): Amended corporate law can incentivize businesses to integrate CSR practices, promoting ethical conduct and responsible corporate citizenship.

(b) Personal Accountability: Introducing provisions that hold individuals accountable for corporate wrongdoing can act as a deterrent against fraudulent practices and encourage responsible decision-making.

(c) Regulatory Collaboration: Closer collaboration between the judiciary and regulatory bodies can foster a proactive approach to compliance and discourage companies from engaging in non-compliant activities.

Streamlining Dispute Resolution Mechanisms:

(a) Encouraging Alternative Dispute Resolution (ADR): Amending corporate law to promote ADR mechanisms can expedite dispute resolution, reducing the burden on the judicial system and minimizing legal expenses for businesses.

(b) Specialized Commercial Courts: Establishing specialized commercial courts with expertise in corporate matters can ensure timely and competent adjudication of corporate disputes.

Legislative Advocacy and Public Awareness:

(a) Advocating Legislative Reforms: The judiciary can play a vital role in advocating for necessary amendments in corporate law, drawing attention to areas requiring modernization and improvement.

(b) Public Awareness Campaigns: Engaging the public and stakeholders through awareness campaigns can foster a culture of compliance and responsible business practices.

Understanding the Need for Amendment Corporate structures should not be used to shield individuals from accountability for their actions. The amendment seeks to address the misuse of corporate entities for fraudulent or harmful purposes, ensuring that perpetrators cannot evade personal responsibility.

Companies Facing Severe Consequences Several high-profile cases have demonstrated the consequences of corporate structures being misused to avoid criminal or civil litigation. One such example is the Enron scandal in the early 2000s, where executives used complex financial structures to conceal losses and deceive shareholders. The company's eventual collapse led to significant legal actions against its executives.

(c) The Role of Corporate Legal Audit: A corporate legal audit is an essential tool for businesses to identify potential legal risks and ensure compliance with relevant laws and regulations. The audit evaluates the company's internal policies, contracts, and corporate governance to detect any areas of vulnerability.

Minimizing Litigation Risk through Legal Audits

(a) Ensuring Compliance: A thorough legal audit ensures that the company complies with all applicable laws, reducing the chances of litigation arising from regulatory violations.

(b) Identifying Risk Areas: The audit helps identify areas prone to legal disputes, such as contract breaches, labor issues, or environmental non-compliance. By addressing these concerns proactively, the company can avoid future litigation.

(c) Improving Corporate Governance: An audit assesses the effectiveness of corporate governance structures, making recommendations for improvements that can enhance transparency and accountability.

Factors Considered in Corporate Law to Prevent Litigation

(a) Transparent Financial Reporting: Accurate and transparent financial reporting reduces the risk of shareholder lawsuits and regulatory investigations.

(b) Robust Internal Controls: Strong internal controls deter fraudulent activities and help identify potential issues before they escalate into full-blown legal disputes.

(c) Ethical Leadership: Companies should foster a culture of ethical conduct from the top down, discouraging illegal or unethical actions by employees and executives.

(d) Shareholder Engagement: Open communication with shareholders can help address concerns and avoid conflicts that might lead to litigation.

Amending corporate law to restrict conversions to criminal or civil litigation is a crucial step in ensuring accountability and fairness within the business landscape. High-profile cases like Enron serve as stark reminders of the consequences of misusing corporate structures. By conducting regular legal audits and considering key factors such as transparent financial reporting, robust internal controls, ethical leadership, and shareholder engagement, companies can minimize the risk of litigation and demonstrate a commitment to responsible business practices. Ultimately, a robust legal framework and ethical corporate conduct will foster a healthier and more sustainable business environment.

To minimize corporate litigation and ensure corporate compliance, the judiciary can take several steps to influence and make changes in corporate law. These steps aim to create a more efficient and effective legal framework for businesses. Here are some key actions the judiciary can take:

Interpretation and Clarification of Existing Laws: The judiciary can play a crucial role in interpreting and clarifying existing corporate laws. By issuing well-reasoned and consistent judgments, the courts can provide guidance to businesses on how to comply with the law and avoid potential legal disputes.

Encouraging Alternative Dispute Resolution (ADR): The judiciary can promote the use of alternative dispute resolution mechanisms, such as mediation and arbitration, to resolve corporate disputes outside the courtroom. ADR can be faster, cost-effective, and less adversarial than traditional litigation, encouraging parties to seek amicable solutions.

Promoting Precedents and Stare Decisis: Consistent application of legal principles through precedents and the principle of stare decisis can provide businesses with a sense of certainty and predictability. It helps stakeholders understand how the law is likely to be applied in various situations, reducing the ambiguity that often leads to litigation.

Holding Individuals Accountable: Judicial decisions that hold individuals accountable for their actions, especially in cases of corporate misconduct, can serve as strong deterrents against unlawful practices. By focusing on personal liability, the judiciary can discourage individuals from misusing corporate structures for wrongful purposes.

Public Interest Litigation (PIL): Encouraging public interest litigation can be a powerful tool to bring to light corporate malpractices that harm the public or society at large. PIL allows concerned citizens and advocacy groups to raise issues of corporate non-compliance, leading to corrective actions and systemic changes.

Collaboration with Regulatory Authorities: The judiciary can collaborate with regulatory authorities and government agencies responsible for overseeing corporate compliance. Working together, they can develop policies and regulations that foster corporate accountability while minimizing unnecessary litigation.

Emphasizing Corporate Social Responsibility (CSR): By recognizing and rewarding companies that actively engage in corporate social responsibility, the judiciary can create incentives for businesses to prioritize ethical behavior and responsible practices.

Timely Disposition of Cases: Efficient and timely resolution of corporate cases can reduce the financial burden on businesses and discourage frivolous litigation. The judiciary can work to streamline court procedures and case management to expedite the resolution of disputes.

Continuing Education for Judges: Providing ongoing education and training for judges in corporate law and related fields ensures that they are well-equipped to handle complex corporate disputes effectively and fairly.

Advocating Legislative Reforms: The judiciary can advocate for necessary legislative reforms in corporate law to address emerging challenges and adapt to changing business dynamics. By identifying gaps in the legal framework, the judiciary can contribute to crafting more comprehensive and relevant laws.

Conclusion:

A proactive judiciary that focuses on interpretation, consistency, and accountability can significantly influence corporate compliance and minimize litigation. By fostering

a legal environment that encourages alternative dispute resolution, personal accountability, and corporate social responsibility, the judiciary can contribute to a fair and efficient corporate legal system that benefits businesses, stakeholders, and society. Need for Amendment in Corporate Law to Minimize Litigation and Ensure Maximum Compliance

□

Chapter II

Retirement Age - Balancing Experience and Renewal

Title: "Beyond Retirement: Exploring Age and Work in a Changing World"

The concept of retirement age is not a one-size-fits-all matter and can vary significantly across different societies and professions. The case of Okinawa in Japan, with its high number of centenarians and no mandatory retirement age, provides a unique perspective on the potential benefits of allowing individuals to work as long as they desire. In contrast, political positions often have an enhanced retirement age, driven by the desire for continuity and stability in governance. However, the retirement age issue goes beyond individual professions and requires a balanced approach to address the diverse needs and challenges of the workforce.

Considering the context of different professions, certain jobs may be physically demanding or require peak cognitive performance, making an extended working life impractical. However, in professions where continued work is feasible and desired by individuals, extending the retirement age might provide not only economic benefits but also a sense of purpose, social engagement, and mental stimulation.

Retirement age in India and Other countries:

The retirement age in the United States varies depending on the specific retirement program you are referring to:

Social Security: The full retirement age for Social Security benefits depends on your birth year. For those born in 1937 or earlier, the full retirement age is 65.

For those born between 1938 and 1960, the full retirement age gradually increases from 65 to 67. For those born in 1960 or later, the full retirement age is 67.

Medicare: The eligibility age for Medicare, the federal health insurance program for people age 65 and older, remains unchanged.

The retirement age in the United Kingdom has undergone significant changes in recent years. The retirement age is gradually increasing due to the government's efforts to address an aging population and rising pension costs. The retirement age in the UK is determined by your gender and birth year, but it is continuously being equalized. Here are the key points:

State Pension Age: The State Pension Age (SPA) is the age at which you become eligible to receive the State Pension. For both men and women, the SPA was 65. However, the SPA has been gradually increasing since 2010.

Equalization of Retirement Age: Prior to April 2010, the retirement age for women was 60, and for men, it was 65. Between April 2010 and November 2018, the SPA for women increased from 60 to 65, gradually equalizing it with men's SPA.

Increasing SPA for Both Genders: The SPA for both men and women has continued to increase in recent years. By November 2018, the SPA for both genders reached 65. The SPA is set to increase further:

By October 2020: The SPA for both genders will increase to 66.

By October 2026: The SPA for both genders will increase to 67.

By April 2037: The SPA for both genders will increase to 68.

The retirement age in Germany has been undergoing changes due to demographic shifts and pension system reforms. The retirement age depends on the type of pension and the year of birth. Here are the key points:

Standard Retirement Age: The standard retirement age for the statutory pension (gesetzliche Rentenversicherung) in Germany is gradually increasing for those born after 1963.

For those born before 1964: The standard retirement age is 65.

For those born between 1964 and 1966: The retirement age gradually increases from 65 years and two months to 65 years and seven months.

For those born in 1967 or later: The retirement age gradually increases from 65 years and eight months to 67 years.

Early Retirement: In Germany, it is possible to retire early, but this may result in reduced pension benefits. Early retirement options are available starting at age 63, but the pension amount may be lower than the full pension available at the standard retirement age.

Flexible Retirement: The German pension system allows for flexible retirement options, which means you can continue to work while receiving a partial pension.

The retirement age in India varies depending on the sector and the specific government or private organization. Here are the general retirement ages for different sectors in India:

Central Government Employees: The retirement age for most central government employees in India is 60 years. There are certain exceptions, where employees in specific government jobs may have different retirement ages.

State Government Employees: The retirement age for state government employees in India is generally 60 years, similar to central government employees. However, some state governments have revised the retirement age to 58 or 59 years in the past.

Private Sector Employees: In the private sector, there is no fixed retirement age mandated by law. The retirement age is usually defined in the employment contract or company policy. It typically ranges between 58 to 65 years, depending on the company and industry.

Armed Forces: The retirement age for personnel in the Indian Armed Forces varies based on rank and service. Generally, officers retire between 54 to 60 years of age, while soldiers retire earlier, usually between 35 to 40 years of age.

Effects:

Retirement in India, like in any other country, can have both positive and negative effects on individuals and society. Here are some of the effects of retirement in India:

- **Financial Impact:** Retirement often leads to a reduction in income, especially for those relying on a pension or savings. While some individuals might have sufficient savings or investments to sustain their lifestyle, others may face financial challenges if they haven't adequately planned for retirement.
- **Change in Lifestyle:** Retirement can bring significant changes in daily routines and lifestyle. Some retirees may find it challenging to adjust

to a more leisurely and less structured life, while others may embrace the newfound freedom.

- **Health and Well-being:** Retirement can have varying effects on health. For some, it may provide an opportunity to focus on personal health and well-being, leading to improved physical and mental health. However, others may experience feelings of isolation and loneliness, which can negatively impact health.
- **Social Engagement:** Retirement can impact an individual's social life. Some retirees might find more time to engage with family and friends, pursue hobbies, or participate in community activities, leading to enhanced social connections. On the other hand, some may face social isolation if they lack a strong social network.
- **Family Dynamics:** Retirement can also influence family dynamics. Some retirees may take on more responsibilities as caregivers for grandchildren or elderly parents, while others may have to adapt to living arrangements with extended family members.
- **Opportunities for New Pursuits:** Retirement can provide individuals with opportunities to explore new interests, hobbies, or even start a new career or business venture. Many retirees in India are increasingly becoming entrepreneurs or pursuing second careers after retirement.
- **Impact on the Workforce:** With an aging population and rising retirement rates, India's workforce might experience shifts in skill availability and labor market dynamics. Some sectors may face a shortage of experienced professionals, while others may see a surge in job

opportunities for younger individuals.

- **Economic Implications:** The retirement of a significant number of experienced professionals can lead to a loss of institutional knowledge and expertise in certain industries. This may necessitate workforce planning and knowledge transfer strategies to ensure a smooth transition.

For politicians, the decision to have an enhanced retirement age should be balanced with the need for new perspectives and fresh ideas. While experience is valuable in politics, the inclusion of younger generations can bring innovation and novel solutions to the ever-changing challenges faced by the nation.

As for other government employees and servants, retirement policies often involve a delicate balance between ensuring the experience and expertise of seasoned workers and creating opportunities for younger individuals to enter the workforce. Extending retirement age for all government employees needs to be carefully evaluated to avoid hindering job opportunities for the youth.

The new order in India increasing the retirement age presents a mix of potential outcomes. On one hand, it may allow experienced employees to continue contributing to their fields, fostering productivity and continuity. On the other hand, it could also limit opportunities for younger individuals and lead to workforce stagnation. Policymakers must consider these implications to strike a balance that benefits both seasoned workers and the younger generation.

Country	Median age	Retirement age
Japan	49.5	62-64
Italy	48.1	62-67
Hong Kong	46.8	60-65
Germany	46.7	60-67
Spain	46.3	65
Greece	46.2	67
Portugal	46.0	66.5
Slovenia	45.9	65
Ukraine	45.3	60
Latvia	45.2	64
Romania	45.1	65
Lithuania	45.0	64
South Korea	45.0	60
Austria	44.8	60-65
Croatia	44.8	62-65
Bulgaria	44.7	61-64
Estonia	44.7	64
Hungary	44.5	65
Bosnia and Herzegovina	44.4	65
Liechtenstein	44.1	64
Switzerland	44.0	64-65
Czechia	43.9	58-62
Serbia	43.7	63.5-65
Finland	43.2	63-68
Malta	43.2	63
Slovakia	42.5	62
Poland	42.4	60-65

Country	Median age	Retirement age
Canada	42.4	60-65
France	42.4	62-67
Cuba	42.3	60-65
Netherlands	42.2	66-68
Denmark	42.2	67
Belgium	41.9	60-65
Belarus	41.7	58-63
Russia	41.5	56.5 61.5
Sweden	41.0	61-67
Thailand	41.0	60
Montenegro	40.7	64-66
United Kingdom	40.6	66
Norway	40.6	62-67
North Macedonia	40.1	62-64
Luxembourg	39.8	65
China	39.8	50-60
Ireland	39.8	66
Singapore	38.9	62-65
United States	38.5	66-70
Georgia	38.0	60-65
Australia	37.9	67
Iceland	37.8	67
New Zealand	37.7	65
Chile	36.6	60-65
Albania	35.8	61-65
United Arab Emirates	35.7	65
Brazil	34.7	62-65

Country	Median age	Retirement age
Sri Lanka	33.9	55
Turkey	33.6	58-60
Iran	33.3	55-60
Argentina	33.0	60-65
Vietnam	32.7	55-60.5
Colombia	32.4	57-62
Saudi Arabia	32.0	60
Kazakhstan	31.7	58-63
Malaysia	31.4	60
Indonesia	31.2	58
Venezuela	30.8	55-60
Mexico	30.6	65
Morocco	30.2	63
Israel	30.1	65-67
India	29.5	60-65
Bangladesh	29.2	63
Nepal	27.1	65
Philippines	25.4	60
Egypt	24.1	60
Pakistan	22.7	60
Cameroon	18.8	50-60
Congo (Dem. Republic)	16.8	58-62

This table shows the Median age and Retirement age of different countries.

Beyond the retirement age itself, it is essential to acknowledge that factors like access to healthcare, overall lifestyle, work conditions, and social support systems also significantly influence an individual's well-being and productivity in their later years. Merely extending the retirement age might not address these broader aspects and their impacts on people's lives.

Conclusion:

The retirement age is a multifaceted issue requiring a nuanced approach that considers the unique demands of various professions, the importance of new perspectives, and the overall well-being of the workforce. While allowing individuals to work as long as they desire can have positive implications, it must be balanced with opportunities for younger generations and comprehensive policies that promote a healthy and sustainable working environment for all. Embracing a diverse and inclusive workforce that leverages the strengths of different age groups will be key to navigating the changing landscape of work and aging in the modern world.

□

Chapter III

Crimes by Juvenile: Addressing Mental Health and Rehabilitation

Title: "A Path to Reformation: Prioritizing Mental Health in Juvenile Rehabilitation"

Introduction:

The chapter delves into the pressing issue of juvenile crimes in India and the need for a comprehensive approach to rehabilitation. It highlights the lack of focus on mental health treatment in Juvenile homes, leading to unaddressed underlying issues and potential recidivism among young offenders. The chapter emphasizes the need to overhaul India's juvenile rehabilitation approach and prioritize mental health analysis and treatment to create a more effective and compassionate juvenile justice system.

Juvenile crime:

In India, child crime is classified as a juvenile crime. That is, delinquent acts committed by children under a specified age are classified as child crimes. However, the question of who should be referred to as a child emerges. Is there a minimum or maximum age requirement for this? Children of various ages have been labelled as child criminals in India. In India, for example, a child must be

14 years old to be declared a criminal, with the maximum age of the same being 18 years. As a result, no general assumptions about the minimum and maximum ages of juvenile offenders exist. Child crime is clearly defined as a crime committed by minors under a certain age. "Child in conflict with law" has been defined under Section 2 (13) of the Juvenile Justice (Care & Protection of Children) Act, 2015 as a child who is alleged or found to have committed an offence and has not completed eighteen years of age on the date of commission of such offence.

Several minor and serious crimes, including theft, burglary, snatching, robbery, dacoity, murder, and rape, are perpetrated on a regular basis throughout India, and the awful fact is that all these crimes are perpetrated by youngsters under the age of eighteen. There is also a trend among minors that those between the ages of 16 and 18 are more likely to be involved in terrible criminal crimes. According to statistics from the National Crime Records Bureau, of the 43,506 offences perpetrated against children under the Indian Penal Code (IPC), 1860 and the Special Local Law (SLL) by juveniles in 2019, 28,830 were committed by individuals of the age range.

Symptoms of a child offender:

In India, authorities charged 27,936 minors in 2012 for their involvement in major crimes such as banditry, murder, rape, and rioting. According to NCRB data, two-thirds (66.6 percent) of individuals who appeared before JJB (Juvenile Justice Boards) in 2012 were between the ages of 16 and 18. Further, 30.9 percent of those surveyed were between the ages of 12 and 16, while the rest (2.5 percent) were between the ages of 7 and 12. There was a 143 percent rise in the number of minor rapes from 2002 to 2012. It also indicated that the number of murders has increased by 87 percent, while the number of women and girls kidnapped by juveniles has increased by 500 percent.

However, between 2007 and 2012, the number of serious crimes like rape and murder perpetrated by juveniles accounted for just 8% of all crimes committed by minors. Petty crimes such as stealing, burglary, and inflicting harm account for 72 percent of all crimes committed by juveniles. Taking into note the increasing graph of juvenile crimes in India, it is necessary to be well familiar with the symptoms being evident to show which child is inclined towards becoming an offender or is already one. The symptoms that can be summarized from various research and studies, responsibly defining a child offender, have been laid down hereunder:

In many cases, a juvenile's bodily structure is healthy, and a healthy body is powerful and courageous.

They are naturally restless, introverted, and disruptive.

They have an unethical, highly emotional, egotistical, and self-centred nature.

They are myopic, oblivious to the repercussions of their actions.

Child offenders are more likely than other youngsters to have a psychotic condition.

In child criminals, there is a lack of healthy id, ego, and superego equilibrium.

They are frequently irritated, disappointed, and melancholic.

They disobey norms, go against the power, break the law, and tend to be untrustworthy.

They have no pre-planned solution to any difficulty that their culture has thrown at them.

In most cases, they don't talk to their relatives and families about their problems.

Types of juvenile crimes in India:

Juvenile crimes manifest themselves in a range of conduct or behaviours. Each pattern has a distinct social setting. According to Yamini Abde, a child rights campaigner, one of the driving motivations behind children being involved in horrible crimes like rape and murder is the desire to do something new, brave, unique, and thrilling. Peer pressure, a need for quick cash, and easy access to crime and pornographic images on the internet increased hostility and sexual activity among teenagers, as well as the awareness that they will not face criminal charges since they are minors, are also catalysts in the process of building a child offender. The lack of fear of punishment has resulted in an increase in the rate of criminality among minors. Howard Becker, in 1966, identified four categories of juvenile delinquency, namely, individual, group-supported, organised, and situational delinquency.

Individual juvenile crimes:

Individual delinquency refers to all delinquent activities undertaken by a juvenile on his or her own. The source of the problem is found inside the criminal themself. Psychiatrists claim that they are the result of psychological issues. The primary cause of these psychological issues is dysfunctional and unhealthy familial contact patterns. The psychiatrists compared the delinquent siblings to their non-delinquent siblings and discovered that the most prevalent reason for committing such crimes was that they were unhappy and dissatisfied with their living conditions.

They engage in delinquent behaviour in the first place to attract attention from family or peers.

Others conduct delinquent activities to alleviate their guilt. Psychiatrists also discovered that delinquents varied from non-delinquent in their relationship with their dads, rather than with their mothers. In addition, their discipline was stricter and more severe.

Circumstantial child crimes:

The core reasons for situational delinquency are not well understood. As a result, regulating such delinquent behaviours is easier than controlling other forms of delinquencies.

Circumstantial delinquency offers a unique viewpoint. The notion is that delinquency is not deeply established and that the motivations for delinquency and the methods for reducing it are frequently straightforward. Because of less developed impulse control and/or lower reinforcement of familial limitations, a young individual engages in delinquent conduct without a profound commitment to delinquency, and because they stand to lose relatively little even if detected.

One researcher who mentions this form of delinquency is David Matza. The idea of circumstantial delinquency is underdeveloped and is not given much weight in the debate over delinquent causation. It is meant to complement rather than replace other kinds.

Organized child crimes:

Organized child crimes are formally structured organisations that commit organised delinquencies. This refers to a system of principles and conventions that drive young people's behaviour when they exhibit delinquent behaviours.

In the 1950s, these delinquencies were studied in the United States, and the term "delinquent sub-culture" was coined. This notion refers to a system of principles and norms that drive group members' conduct to stimulate the performance of delinquent activities, grant status based on such acts, and define typical connections for those who fall outside of the groups defined by group norms.

Group supported child crimes:

Delinquencies are committed in this sort in the company of others, and the cause is found not in the individual's personality or in the delinquent's family, but in the culture of the individual's home and neighbourhood.

This sort of delinquency is discussed in Thrasher, Shaw, and McKay's research. According to research, most young children who turned delinquent did so as a result of their affiliation and companionship with other delinquents.

Unlike psychogenic theories, this group of concepts focuses on what is learned and from whom it is learned, rather than the difficulties that may lead to delinquency motivation.

Reasons behind juvenile crimes in India:

No one is born with the potential to be a criminal. Circumstances have shaped them into who they are. The socio-cultural environment, both within and outside of one's household, has a big influence on one's life and general personality. The causes of juvenile crimes, according to Healy and Bronner, are bad company, adolescent instability and impulses, early sex experience, mental conflicts, extreme social suggestibility, love of adventure, motion picture, school dissatisfaction, poor recreation, street life, vocational dissatisfaction, impulse, and physical conditions of various kinds. However, in India, it is poverty and the impact of the media, particularly social media, that encourages youths to engage in illegal activity. Poverty is one of the leading factors of a child's involvement in criminal activity. Also, the current function of social media, which has a more destructive impact on young brains.

Socio-economic reasons:

Broken homes:

According to one of Uday Shankar's research in India, 13.3 percent of the 140 juveniles came from broken households. Death of one or both parents, chronic sickness or insanity, desertion, or divorce can all break up a family. Interaction at home is a critical component of a child's socialisation.

Poverty:

A substantial percentage of delinquent youngsters originate from low-income families. They perpetuate their crimes as gang members. According to Uday Shankar's research, 83 percent of youngsters originate from low-income homes. Poverty forces both parents to work outside the home for lengthy periods of time to earn their daily bread. There will be no one to look after the children. Such youngsters may join up with gangsters, either knowingly or unconsciously, and become criminals.

Friends and companions:

As the child grows older, he/she ventures out into the neighbourhood and joins a playgroup or peer group. He/ she will very certainly become a delinquent if he/she joins a group or gang that supports delinquent tendencies. Adolescents also commit crimes because of poor friendships. According to studies, delinquent behaviours are committed in groups. Shaw examined 6000 youths involved in criminality in his Illinois Crime Survey of 1928. In 90% of the instances, he discovered that two or more youths were involved in the crime.

Beggary:

Juvenile misbehaviour is frequently caused by beggars. Most child beggars originate from either very impoverished backgrounds or shattered homes. These youngsters are robbed of their parents' much-needed love and attention. They realise that the only way to satisfy their wants and meet their requirements is to engage in deviant behaviour. As a result, they become delinquents.

Analysis:

The chapter begins by pointing out the stark contrast between developed countries and India in their approach to juvenile rehabilitation. While reformative homes in developed countries prioritize mental health analysis and treatment, many Juvenile homes in India primarily engage young offenders in hard work to earn their livelihood, overlooking the root causes of their criminal behaviour.

The chapter further highlights the consequences of inadequate rehabilitation, where many juvenile offenders await the completion of their term without receiving essential mental health support or comprehensive rehabilitation. This failure to address underlying issues may contribute to a higher recurrence of criminal behaviour upon release.

The chapter sheds light on the disturbing reality that a significant number of rape cases involve juvenile offenders, as revealed by a study by the National Crime Records Bureau in 2017.

Recommendations for Effective Rehabilitation:

To address the issue effectively, the chapter proposes a holistic rehabilitation approach that considers various factors contributing to juvenile criminal behaviour. Key recommendations include:

Prioritizing Mental Health Analysis and Treatment: Juvenile homes should emphasize mental health assessment and treatment as a core aspect of their reformation programs. Addressing mental health issues can be instrumental in reducing recidivism and fostering positive transformation.

Education and Skill Development: Providing education and skill development opportunities to young offenders can empower them with knowledge and critical thinking skills, enhancing their chances of leading productive lives upon release.

Counselling and Therapy: Offering counselling and therapeutic interventions can help juvenile offenders understand the consequences of their actions, develop empathy, and take responsibility for their behaviour. Additionally, these interventions can help them cope with trauma or adverse experiences that may have contributed to their criminal behaviour.

Restorative Justice: Emphasizing restorative justice practices can encourage young offenders to make amends to victims and repair harm to the community, promoting meaningful rehabilitation.

Minor Rapist in Bihar:

Juvenile justice board (JJB) in Bihar gave a decision in a case of raping and impregnating a minor under IPC Section 376 and Protection of Children from Sexual Offences (POCSO) Act. The accused who was 13 years old raped a 12-year-old girl while she was carrying food for her father who used to work in an agricultural field. Due to fear, the girl did not inform anybody about the incident. The case came into light when the girl was found to be pregnant with severe pain in her lower abdomen. A case was registered by the girl's aunt and the accused was arrested. Later, he was taken into custody and sent to a Patna based remand home. The impact on the girl was severe as the family refused to accept her and drove her away. She was shifted to a shelter home where she delivered the baby.

The Nirbhaya Gang Rape Case, 2012:

The landmark judgement of the NIRBHAYA GANG RAPE CASE, 2012 which shook and left the entire nation speechless was a nail in the coffin of the needed changes in the system of law and delivery of justice related to the crimes committed by minors.

The Supreme Court upheld the capital punishment for the four convicts – Akshay Thakur, Vinay Sharma, Pawan Gupta, and Mukesh labelling the act as barbaric and devilish. The fifth accused member of the gangrape accused, Ram Singh was found hanging in his cell in Tihar jail in 2013 while the sixth minor member was just sent to the reformation facility for 3 years. He was sent to a correction home for three years in North Delhi's Majnu Ka Tila instead of punishment with the others due to his minor age after he was found guilty in the infamous Delhi Gangrape Case. Despite, accusations of being the most brutal out of the six and attacking the victim severely with an iron rod, he was relieved of capital punishment and the allegations were brushed away by the Juvenile Justice board.

Considering these complex considerations, it is vital to adopt a comprehensive approach to juvenile justice that addresses the underlying issues contributing to juvenile crime. This includes ensuring access to mental health services, education, and skill development within the juvenile justice system. Restorative justice programs can also play a role in promoting empathy and understanding while holding juveniles accountable for their actions.

While acknowledging the gravity of heinous crimes,

it is crucial to strike a balance between punishment and rehabilitation, focusing on the well-being and potential for positive transformation in young offenders. Public discussions and evidence-based approaches are essential in shaping an effective and compassionate juvenile justice system that upholds both justice and human rights.

Most serious offense	Number of juvenile arrests
All offenses	424,300
Murder and nonnegligent manslaughter	930
Rape	NA
Robbery	12,000
Aggravated assault	19,140
Burglary	15,130
Larceny-theft	46,700
Motor vehicle theft	11,660
Arson	1,200
Simple assault	70,940
Forgery and counterfeiting	470
Fraud	2,620
Embezzlement	430
Stolen property (buying, receiving, possessing)	8,190
Vandalism	23,130
Weapons (carrying, possessing, etc.)	11,110

Most serious offense	Number of juvenile arrests
Prostitution and commercialized vice	110
Sex offenses (except rape & prostitution)	NA
Drug abuse violations	42,280
Gambling	70
Offenses against the family and children	2,420
Driving under the influence	5,870
Liquor laws	17,910
Drunkenness	2,390
Disorderly conduct	24,720
Vagrancy	250
All other offenses (except traffic)	85,970
Curfew and loitering	11,680
Violent Crime Index	NA
Property Crime Index	74,680
Violent crimes*	32,070

This table shows the number of Juveniles arrested yearly.

Conclusion:

The chapter concludes by emphasizing the significance of addressing the root causes of criminal behaviour in juvenile offenders to prevent future offenses and promote societal well-being. Prioritizing mental health treatment, comprehensive rehabilitation, education, and skill development are vital steps towards creating an effective juvenile justice system.

The alarming number of rape cases involving juvenile offenders underscores the urgency of the issue. Early intervention and prevention programs that educate young individuals about consent, gender equality, and respectful relationships are essential to tackle this problem proactively.

Ultimately, creating a juvenile justice system that focuses on mental health support and comprehensive rehabilitation while addressing societal issues can foster a safer, more compassionate society. By providing young offenders with a path to reformation, India can contribute to reducing recidivism rates and promoting a brighter future for all.

□

Chapter IV

Legalization of Sex Workers: Balancing Controversy and Societal Impact

Title: "Beyond Taboos: Exploring the Case for Legalizing Sex Work in India"

Introduction:

This chapter delves into the contentious topic of legalizing sex work in India, acknowledging the social taboo and illegal status associated with prostitution. It highlights the prevalence of illegal trafficking and the potential benefits of legalizing sex work, such as curbing human trafficking, improving public health, and contributing to the economy. However, it also considers the ethical and moral concerns and potential negative consequences, calling for a comprehensive evaluation of the societal impact before making any decisions.

Analysis:

The chapter begins by acknowledging the illegal and stigmatized nature of sex work in India. Despite its illegal status, red-light areas in certain cities are not strictly intervened. It then explores the prevalence of rape cases in India, emphasizing the urgent need to address the underlying issues leading to such crimes.

The chapter examines the potential benefits of legalizing sex work, such as reducing human trafficking, curbing the spread of HIV and other sexually transmitted infections, improving public health and safety for sex workers, and contributing significantly to the economy through taxation and formalization.

On the other hand, it also presents counterarguments against legalization, including ethical concerns about the exploitative nature of sex work, worries about increased demand and commodification of human beings, and the potential for normalization and moral hazard.

Prostitution In India:

Sex workers face continuous brutality, violence from clients and banishment from every community activity and even their own family. The recent release of the movie Gangubai Kathiawadi, which revolves around the life of a sex worker turned campaigner has once again brought the topic into the spotlight.

Let us understand the grey areas where sex workers live, and prostitution takes place.

History:

During 300 C.E., it was an established custom of purchasing young girls and dedicating them to temples. They were offered as objects of sexual pleasure for the temple and priests. It was commonly practised and termed as the 'Devadasi System'. The custom later developed and now the girls came to be known as the 'Brides of the Town' or 'Nagarvadhu'. They did not marry and considered God as their husband.

These women were considered pure, and no one touched them. But after the Britishers came, the life of these women changed. The Devadasi's were forced to perform dance and music for the British officials. Later they were even to be called for the sexual pleasures of the officers. The status of the Devadasi changed completely into the role of prostitutes. Soon women started selling their bodies in exchange for money and this led to the growth of prostitution activities in India.

There are as many as above 20 million commercial sex workers in India.

Is Prostitution legal in India?

The countries like New Zealand, Australia, Austria, Netherlands have regularized the practice of prostitution by formulating specific rules. But on the other hand, countries like Kenya, Morocco and Afghanistan have declared it illegal. The position in India is somewhat in between these two extreme ends and it has made prostitution legal, subject to certain limitations and restrictions.

To point out that the words prostitution as such has not been made punishable but there are certain activities related to it like, running brothels, soliciting, trafficking, and pimping are considered as a punishable offence under the Immoral Traffic (Prevention) Act, 1956. For instance, if an individual engages in the activity of trafficking, the same shall be a punishable act but if the same individual receives consideration in exchange for sex might not be punishable. We can find that the centre of the topic resides in a grey area.

What are the laws regarding Prostitution?

- As per Section 2(f) of the Immoral Traffic (Prevention) Act, 1956 prostitution means 'the sexual exploitation or abuse of persons for commercial purpose'.

- Article 23 of the Constitution prohibits traffic in human beings and beggars and other similar forms of forced labour.
- Sections 372 and 373 specifically deals with child prostitution. According to it, whoever sells, lets to hire, or disposes of any person who is a minor to be used for any illicit or immoral purpose or for prostitution shall be liable for punishment. Such punishment may extend to 10 years. Section 373 punishes the person who buys minors for the purposes of prostitution or illicit intercourse for 10 years and is liable for a fine.
- Sections 366A, 366B, 370A of the IPC punish the procreation of minor girls, importation of girls from foreign for sex and exploitation of a trafficked person respectively. The Code has only limited provisions dealing with prostitution.

Recognized Rights of the Prostitutes:

The Constitution treats prostitutes at par with the citizens of the country and hence are entitled to all the rights as that of citizens of India.

The situation of prostitutes came to light for the first time in the case of Buddhadeb Karm Askar vs State of West Bengal, wherein the accused murdered a sex worker. The apex court to this recognized the plight of prostitutes and held that prostitutes are human beings, and none has the right to assault or murder them. The court made remarkable point 'women indulge in prostitution not only for pleasure but out of poverty'. Thus, Court made directions to the Government for making schemes to give vocational training to sex workers across the country.

The Bombay High Court in Kajal Mukesh Singh & Ors v. State of Maharashtra, dealt with three women in their late twenties who were picked by the police and booked under the Act. The court has held that 'an adult women shall have all fundamental rights and to choose their occupation'.

Punishment and Penalty:

The activities considered illegal under the Immoral Traffic (Prevention) Act, 1956 have been charged with heavy punishments. As pointed above, the activity of prostitution or sex appeal is not punished but the activities surrounding it have been made punishable under the Act. The minimum sentence for brothel-keeping is one-year along with a fine. A minimum term of seven years can be imposed for the offence of procuring a girl child for prostitution, which may even extend to life imprisonment. Punishment of an offender for the exploitation of a trafficked minor is somewhere between five to seven years.

Positive Initiatives:

The Ministry of Women and Child Development has launched its 'Ujjawalla' scheme, whereby the sex workers are identified, and are prevented, rescued, rehabilitated, reintegrated, and repatriated from trafficking and commercial sexual exploitation. They also came up with a financial assistance programme to help themselves with the basic amenities of life.

The sex workers collectively working for the National Network of Sex Workers (NNSW) aims to provide a voice to the issues faced by sex workers at all major forums. They also work to address myths, misconceptions and stigmas that degrade the position of sex workers and create situations for abuse against them.

Recently the apex court directed State Government/ Union Territories to implement the issuance of ration cards/Voters Identity cards and upon the same, the UIDAI has accepted that no formal proof of residence shall be required to issue Aadhar cards for sex workers.

Only a handful of sex workers have a birth certificate or any kind of identity certificate. They face discrimination at every level of society, be it in medical, educational, or cultural places. They lack an identity of their own. All these laws and systems in practice have put the lives of sex workers in a grey light. The Government have created the 'red-light areas', both for their personal and professional sustenance. This makes it hard for them to find clients and puts them in a state of fear of being caught by police and harassed and an increased chance of being misbehaved. They are hardly treated as an equal part of society. Individuals from the privileged class need to come forward and help sex workers get the status of what they deserve.

It is emphasized that any consideration of legalization must be done with a comprehensive approach, considering the broader societal and cultural context. Public opinion, the influence of stakeholders, and the existing legal framework all play significant roles in shaping policies related to sex work.

Rape at the national level, number of police-recorded offences, in per 100,000 inhabitants

Country/territory	Total count (Rate per 100,000 population)
Mauritius	3.9
Uganda	2.1
Botswana	92.9
Senegal	5.6
Bahamas	22.7

Country/territory	Total count (Rate per 100,000 population)
Grenada	30.6
Jamaica	24.4
Saint Kitts and Nevis	28.6
Saint Vincent and the Grenadines	25.6
Belize	6.7
El Salvador	11.0
Mexico	13.2
Nicaragua	31.6
Panama	28.3
Bolivia	26.1
Colombia	6.8
Guyana	15.5
Canada	1.7
United States of America	27.3
Kyrgyzstan	5.9
Hong Kong	1.6
Japan	1.0
Mongolia	12.4
Republic of Korea	13.6
Thailand	6.7

Country/territory	Total count (Rate per 100,000 population)
India	0.45
Armenia	0.4
Azerbaijan	0.2
Georgia	1.9
Bulgaria	2.8
Hungary	2.5
Poland	4.1
Republic of Moldova	10.3
Russian Federation	3.4
Ukraine	1.4
Estonia	6.0
Finland	15.2
Ireland	10.7
Latvia	3.5
Lithuania	6.3
Norway	19.2
Sweden	63.5
Albania	0.7
Andorra	1.2
Bosnia and Herzegovina	1.2
Croatia	3.2

Country/territory	Total count (Rate per 100,000 population)
Greece	1.9
Malta	2.6
Portugal	4.0
Serbia	0.7
Slovenia	3.1
Spain	3.4
Austria	10.4
Belgium	27.9
Germany	9.4
Liechtenstein	0.0
Netherlands	9.2
Switzerland	7.1
Australia	28.6
New Zealand	25.8
South Africa	95.9

This table shows the number of rape count over 100,000 population.

Conclusion:

The chapter concludes by acknowledging the complexity of the issue and the need for careful consideration before making any decisions on the legalization of sex work in India. While there are potential benefits, including curbing human trafficking, improving public health, and boosting the economy, there are also ethical concerns and potential negative consequences to consider.

If India were to consider legalizing sex work, it must also invest in comprehensive support services to address potential consequences and ensure the safety and well-being of sex workers. Robust regulation and continuous evaluation would be necessary to mitigate negative outcomes and maximize potential benefits.

Ultimately, the decision on legalizing sex work should be based on thorough research, evidence-based policy-making, and consideration of the societal impact. Open dialogues and engagement with various stakeholders, including sex workers themselves, would be essential in shaping a balanced and ethical approach to address this sensitive and complex issue.

□

Chapter V

Upholding Integrity: The Battle Against Corruption and Corrupt Practices

Title: "Towards a Transparent Future: The Fight Against Corruption"

Introduction:

This chapter delves into the critical aspect of combating corruption and corrupt practices in governance and legal systems around the world. Corruption, the misuse of power for personal gain, poses severe consequences for society, ranging from income inequality to weakened democracy and hindrance to economic development. The chapter emphasizes the need for effective legal measures and strict penalties to deter individuals from engaging in corrupt practices.

Analysis:

The chapter begins by shedding light on the widespread prevalence of corruption in various sectors, including public services, politics, and corporate realms. The consequences of corruption go beyond financial losses, affecting the quality of projects, infrastructure, and public services.

The chapter emphasizes that corruption undermines basic monitoring mechanisms, making it challenging to gauge or monitor project implementation. It fosters a culture of shortcuts and undermines merit-based systems, perpetuating inefficiencies and compromising the quality of work.

The political arena is not immune to corruption, as vast sums of money spent on elections may later lead to seeking personal gains through corrupt means. The chapter highlights the importance of considering candidates' qualifications, past records, and contributions to society when running for public office.

To address corruption effectively, the chapter advocates for standardized laws and the adoption of successful anti-corruption measures from other countries, such as the United Kingdom. However, implementing these changes requires political will, societal awareness, and a robust legal framework.

Recommendations for Combating Corruption:

Strong Laws and Penalties: Implementing stringent laws and imposing severe penalties on corrupt individuals can serve as a deterrent and set an example for others.

Effective Enforcement: Ensuring effective enforcement of anti-corruption laws through an independent and impartial judiciary is essential for holding wrongdoers accountable.

Public Awareness Campaigns: Educating the public about the detrimental impact of corruption and promoting transparency and ethical behaviour can foster a culture of integrity.

Promoting Transparency and Accountability: Encouraging transparency in governance and decision-making processes can help prevent corruption and ensure accountability.

- AIR 1973 SC 913 at pp-915-20= 1973 Cr LJ 902
  A.C. Sharma V. Delhi Administration

In this case the question was whether with the setting up of the Delhi Special Police Establishment (i.e., CBI) The Anti-Corruption Branch of Delhi Police had been completely deprived of its power to investigate into the corruption cases against Central Government servants or whether both the SPE and Anti-Corruption Branch to had power to investigate, it been a matter of internal administrative arrangement for the appropriate authority to regulate the assignment of the investigation of the case according to the exigencies of the situation. The Supreme Court held that the scheme of DSPE Act 1946 does not either expressly or by necessary implication divest the regular police authority of their jurisdiction, power and competent to investigate into offences under any other competent law.

- 2004 Cr.L.R. SC 242
  State of Maharasthra V. Gajanan & Anr.

P.C. Act 1988 - Sec. 7 – Criminal Procedure Code 1973 – Sec. 389(1) – Conviction in corruption case- Stay of sentence as well as conviction by High Court thus facilitating continuance of service of respondent public servant – Held, not proper. impugned order set aside. (See Para 4) Ref. 2001 CrLR SC 526 K.C. Sareen V. CBI Chandigarh. In this case the Hon'ble Supreme Court had that by the impugned judgment the High Court while entertaining a criminal appeal against an order of conviction recorded by the Special Court against the respondents herein for an offence u/s 7 of the P.C. Act not only State the sentence imposed by the trial court but also proceeded to stay the conviction which could facilitate the respondent public servant to continue the hold the civil post in spite of the conviction recorded against him. While doing so the High Court rejected the objection of the state as also distinguished the judgment of this court in K.C. Sareen V. CBI Chandigarh.

In the said judgment in K.C. Sareen (Supra), The Hon'ble Supreme Court has held that it is only in very exceptional cases that the court should exercise such power of stay in matters arising out of the act. The High Court has in the impugned order nowhere pointed out what is exceptional fact that in its opinion required it to stay the conviction. The impugned order was set aside and the appeals were allowed.

- 1998 Cr.L.J. Delhi Page 3022
  Teka Ram Appellant V. The State Respondent

P.C. Act 1947 Sec. 5(1)(d) - Illegal gratification - Conviction for - Validity - Trap Case - Accused, a reader in court demanding bribe for forwarding application - Slipping away from court when trap was laid - thereby he could neither be apprehended nor tainted money could be recovered - Accused cannot benefit from said circumstance to claim discrepancy in investigation- Offence against accused proved beyond doubt - Conviction upheld.

- 2005 Cr.L.J. Bombay 2868
  CBI, New Delhi V. Abdul Karim Telgi & others.

Evidence Act Sections 8, 45 - Application for permission to record voice sample of accused - For purpose of identification of his voice to compare it with tape recorded telephonic conversation - Requiring accused to record his voice sample - does not infringe article 20(3) of Constitution as it does not amount " Testimonial Compulsion" In such a case, even if the subject application seeking for direction to accused to give his voice sample as filed by the investigating agency before the court makes no reference to any specification provision of law even so it is not a case of no jurisdiction to consider such application or grant to said relief. If such direction were to be granted and the accused resisted or refused to co-operate, the consequence thereof is provided under Sec. 6 of the Act 1920. This obviously may be in addition to the adverse influence that can be drawn against the obstinate accused. (para 14)

- AIR 1996 SC 186
  SP CBI appellant V. Deepak Chaudhary and others Respondents

P.C. Act 1947 – Sec. 6 – Sanction for Prosecution – Validity – Grant of Sanction is an administrative function– Opportunity of hearing to accused before according sanction need not be given.

P.C. Act 1947 – Sec. 6 - Sanction for Prosecution – Validity – Order quashing sanction on ground that accused was exonerated of charge by disciplinary authority – not proper.

- 2001 Cr.L.J. (Kerala) 4448
  Ahamed Kalnad V. State of Kerala

P.C. Act 1988, Sections 13, 19- Sanction for Prosecution-Common Sanction order passed for more than 25 accused – Offences involves in all cases similar and part of alleged larger conspiracy- passing common order justified and valid.

Para 7 – Even if the Engineers concerned could have been removed from service only by their head of department there cannot be any bar to the government itself deciding to issue of Sanction for Prosecution in so far as the government is superior authority vis-a-vis the Head of Department.

- 2005 Cr.L.J. NOC (Rajasthan) 256

Ravi Shankar Srivastava V. State of Rajasthan & others.

Constitution of India, art. 226 – Prevention of Corruption Act 1988, Sec. 13 – DSPE Act 1946, Sec. 6-A-Quashing of FIR – Allegation in FIR that petitioner working as Member, Board of Revenue was habitually accepting illegal gratification and that illegal benefit was to be granted by him by passing a review order in a particular revenue matter- Enquiry and Verification with regard to source information is permissible before lodging of FIR – Evidence collected in support of FIR also discloses commission of offence- FIR cannot be quashed.

Corruption Perceptions Index table

Nation or Territory	
	Score
Afghanistan	24
Albania	36
Algeria	33
Angola	33
Argentina	38
Armenia	46
Australia	75
Austria	71

Nation or Territory	Score
Azerbaijan	23
Bahamas	64
Bahrain	44
Bangladesh	25
Barbados	65
Belarus	39
Belgium	73
Benin	43
Bhutan	68
Bolivia	31
Bosnia and Herzegovina	34
Botswana	60
Brazil	38
Bulgaria	43
Burkina Faso	42
Burundi	17
Cambodia	24
Cameroon	26
Canada	74
Cape Verde	60
Central African Republic	24
Chad	19

Nation or Territory	
	Score
Chile	67
China	45
Colombia	39
Comoros	19
Congo	21
Costa Rica	54
Croatia	50
Cuba	45
Cyprus	52
Czechia	56
Democratic Republic of the Congo	20
Denmark	90
Djibouti	30
Dominica	55
Dominican Republic	32
Ecuador	36
Egypt	30
El Salvador	33
Equatorial Guinea	17
Eritrea	22
Estonia	74
Eswatini	30

Nation or Territory	Score
Ethiopia	38
Fiji	53
Finland	87
France	72
Gabon	29
Gambia	34
Georgia	56
Germany	79
Ghana	43
Greece	52
Grenada	52
Guatemala	24
Guinea	25
Guinea-Bissau	21
Guyana	40
Haiti	17
Honduras	23
Hong Kong	76
Hungary	42
Iceland	74
India	40
Indonesia	34

Nation or Territory	Score
Iran	25
Iraq	23
Ireland	77
Israel	63
Italy	56
Ivory Coast	37
Jamaica	44
Japan	73
Jordan	47
Kazakhstan	36
Kenya	32
Kosovo	41
Kuwait	42
Kyrgyzstan	27
Laos	31
Latvia	59
Lebanon	24
Lesotho	37
Liberia	26
Libya	17
Lithuania	62
Luxembourg	77

Nation or Territory	
	Score
Madagascar	26
Malawi	34
Malaysia	47
Maldives	40
Mali	28
Malta	51
Mauritania	30
Mauritius	50
Mexico	31
Moldova	39
Mongolia	33
Montenegro	45
Morocco	38
Mozambique	26
Myanmar	23
Namibia	49
Nepal	34
Netherlands	80
New Zealand	87
Nicaragua	19
Niger	32
Nigeria	24

Nation or Territory	Score
North Korea	17
North Macedonia	40
Norway	84
Oman	44
Pakistan	27
Panama	36
Papua New Guinea	30
Paraguay	28
Peru	36
Philippines	33
Poland	55
Portugal	62
Qatar	58
Romania	46
Russia	28
Rwanda	51
Saint Lucia	55
Saint Vincent and the Grenadines	60
São Tomé and Príncipe	45
Saudi Arabia	51
Senegal	43
Serbia	36

Nation or Territory	
	Score
Seychelles	70
Sierra Leone	34
Singapore	83
Slovakia	53
Slovenia	56
Solomon Islands	42
Somalia	12
South Africa	43
South Korea	63
South Sudan	13
Spain	60
Sri Lanka	36
Sudan	22
Suriname	40
Sweden	83
Switzerland	82
Syria	13
Taiwan	68
Tajikistan	24
Tanzania	38
Thailand	36
Timor-Leste	42

Nation or Territory	Score
Togo	30
Trinidad and Tobago	42
Tunisia	40
Turkey	36
Turkmenistan	19
Uganda	26
Ukraine	33
United Arab Emirates	67
United Kingdom	73
United States	69
Uruguay	74
Uzbekistan	31
Vanuatu	48
Venezuela	14
Vietnam	42
Yemen	16
Zambia	33
Zimbabwe	23

This table shows the corruption rate in different countries.

Conclusion:

The chapter concludes by highlighting the significance of combating corruption through a multi-pronged approach.

It is essential to adopt strong laws, enforce them effectively, and promote transparency and accountability in all sectors of society. Public awareness campaigns play a crucial role in fostering a culture of integrity and ethical behaviour.

Ultimately, the fight against corruption requires collective efforts from governments, institutions, civil society, and individuals. By upholding integrity and taking a stand against corrupt practices, societies can move towards a transparent and equitable future, ensuring a just and prosperous environment for all.

□

Chapter VI

A Call for Change

Title: "Democracy in Transition: Towards Qualifications and Accountability in Politics"

As professionals, we understand the importance of qualifications and expertise in various fields. Just as doctors, lawyers, and accountants need specialized training to provide competent services, politicians also require a level of knowledge and understanding to govern effectively. While experience can be valuable, it should not be the sole criterion for political candidacy. An inclusive approach to political representation should encourage a mix of experienced leaders and fresh minds with the necessary qualifications.

However, in reality, political appointments often seem to be influenced by favouritism and nepotism rather than merit and capabilities. Some individuals secure positions without the necessary experience, and this raises concerns about their ability to govern a state, district, or region responsibly.

The lack of a monitoring/supervising authority for political candidates' selection and performance exacerbates the problem. Without proper checks and balances, politicians might misuse their positions for personal gain rather than working for the betterment of society. Instances of corruption and misuse of power undermine citizens' trust in the democratic process.

To address these issues, it is crucial to establish a more transparent and accountable system for selecting political candidates. One possible solution is to involve a committee comprising people from various political parties and retired judges to evaluate potential candidates based on their merits and reputation in society. Such a committee could help prevent favouritism and nepotism in the selection process and ensure that qualified and deserving individuals are given the opportunity to serve the nation.

Moreover, introducing a monitoring mechanism to oversee the performance of elected leaders is essential. This can be achieved through an independent body or a strengthened judiciary system. Accountability should be a fundamental aspect of political leadership, and those who fail to deliver on their promises or engage in corrupt practices should be held responsible for their actions.

To ensure a more responsible use of funds and resources, political campaigns should be conducted within reasonable financial limits. Allocating excessive amounts of money for rallies and elections while neglecting essential agencies during emergencies is not in the spirit of democracy. Striking a balance between campaigning and responsible governance is necessary for a healthy democratic process.

The scenario since decades:

The Constitution of India came into force on 26th January, 1950. It is the second largest country by area, the second most populated country after China, and has the most populated democracy in the world. Modern humans came to India from Africa around 55,000 years back. India is the home for all religions. In the early medieval times, Christianism, Islam and Zoroastrians have put down roots on India's southern and western coasts. Our country is known as the Secular, Federal, Republic and is basically governed in a democratic parliamentary system. It is a Nuclear Weapons state which actually ranks high in military power. India has managed quite well in lowering the poverty rate through raising the cost of increasing economic equality. Our country is well known for its vast culture, peace and harmony. From South Indians to Punjabis to Muslims, we have a wide range of cultures. The motto of our country is "Satyameva Jayate".

The Government India is totally governed according to the Constitution which is our country's supreme document. All rules and regulations which are framed over there are amended by the citizens and if any of it is violated then they approach the court and hence seek justice. The constitution stated India to be "sovereign, democratic, republic". Our government is "quasi federal" which includes strong center but weak states. The country has grown to be federal since the beginning of 1990s. As discussed earlier, our government includes three branches i.e. Executive, Legislature and Judiciary. Our country has a well-known political background with politicians who take a lead role in various states, playing various roles and also using their logic so as to benefit common people. The Government of India is located in New Delhi, which is known as our National Capital.

Political System of India:

The Political System of India is totally governed by the Constitution of India. As we know that our country is a federal democratic republic in which The President of India is the head of the state and the Prime Minister is the head of the Government. The constitution clearly defines all the organizational powers of the center and state government which is totally supreme i.e. all the laws of the nation must be according to the provisions given in the constitution. There are 2 houses i.e. Lok Sabha (House of the People) and Rajya Sabha (Council of States) which fully represents the people of India as a whole. Lok Sabha has around 543 members elected from 543 Indian Constituencies. Whereas, in Rajya Sabha there are around 245 members out of which 233 members are elected through elections and the remaining 12 members are elected by The President. The elections in our country take place at a term of every 5 years. The first election in our state took place in the year 1951 which was won by Indian National Congress, who dominated the government till 1977. After that a new government was formed. In the year 2014 Bhartiya Janata Party came into force which again brought back the rule of a single party. In the year 2019 the "Economist Intelligence Unit" rated India as a flawed democracy.

The states actually have their own legislation. Some have two houses and some have just one house. The house where the legislative matters take place is called Vidhan Sabha. In the state elections members of the lower house are elected. The Supreme Court is the supreme body of our country. As the time has passed, we have seen that there have been vast changes in the Democracy of our country. From a multi fold increase in the size of the middle class to penetration of social media, we have seen a lot of changes.

The social and geographical expansion of the Bharatiya Janata Party (BJP) since 2014 altered the entire political landscape resulting in further marginalisation of the Congress, the decimation of the Left Front, and a huge reduction in the power of state-level parties. Similarly, as the BJP made huge profits across the board, various voting blocs curated in the past along lines of caste and class also seem to have melted in saffron colour.

Elections in India:

The Elections are carried on according with a parliamentary system, governed by the Constitution. The constitution mentions all the powers which have to be distributed between the centre and the states. As we all know that The President of India is the main head of our country and Supreme Commander in Chief for all defence forces. However, the Prime Minister of India, is the leader of the party or political alliance having majority in the national elections to the Lok Sabha, which exercises most executive powers for the matters that require nationwide affection under a federal system. Our country is divided into states. Each state has a Chief Minister who is a leader of the party or political alliance who has won a majority of votes at the state elections or known as state assembly elections.

The elections are controlled by the Election Commission which is a federal body governed by the provisions of the constitution. The main tasks of the commission are to monitor and administer all the electoral process of India. This body is responsible to ensure that elections are free and fair, without any degree of unfairness anytime. Commission ensures that the conduct of members pre-elections, during elections and post-elections are according to the statutory legislations. Elections in the Republic of India include elections for:

- Members of Parliament in the Lok Sabha;
- Members of State Legislative Assemblies all over;
- Members of the Parliament in the Rajya Sabha;

- Members of State Legislative Council;
- Members in Village Panchayats;

By-election is held when a person of a particular constituent dies, resigns, or is disqualified.

If a candidate wants to contest at the election, then he/ she has to submit their nomination papers to the election commission. After scrutinising all the papers, a list of all the candidates is published. No party should use the resources by the government for any election campaigns. Also, no party should bribe the other candidates. If all such things come under the notice of the commission, then the nomination of that particular candidate is cancelled. Usually, the campaigning of elections ends two days before the polling day. Government officers are made in-charge of all the election processes. EVMs are used instead of Ballot Boxes so as to prevent any such fraud. After a citizen votes his or her left index finger is marked with an indelible ink. This practice was adopted in the year 1962.

Political Parties of India:

India, has been the largest democracy the world has seen since 200 political parties were formed, since it attained Independence in the year 1947. As compared to other democracies, India consists of a large number of political parties and some of them are woven around their leaders. The two main parties in India are the Congress and BJP, which dominate national politics. At this present scenario we have around seven national parties, and many state parties.

Every political party in India irrespective of national or state must have a symbol and must be registered with Election Commission of India. Symbols are used for the parties so as to identify political parties so that illiterate people can vote by recognizing the party symbols. In the current scenarios, the Commission has framed the following five principles:

- A party, or State, must have a legislative presence.
- A National party's legislative presence must be in Lok Sabha. A State party's legislative presence must be in the State Assembly.
- A party can set up a candidate only amongst its own members.
- A party that loses its recognition shall not lose its symbol immediately but shall be allowed to use that symbol for some time to try and retrieve its status.

Recognition should be given to a party only on the basis of their performance at the elections and not because it is a small or thin group of some other recognized party.

As compared to other democracy, political parties represent different societies among the Indian Society and the region, and the values by them have also played a key role during the elections. The political parties represent the executive and legislative branch of the government. The people of India by using their power to vote choose their representatives. If a party fails to earn a majority at the elections, then they used to form a coalition.

India has a multi-party system, where there are numerous national as well as regional parties. A regional party may gain a majority and rule a particular state. If a party rules at more than 4 states, then it is called a National Party. Out of 72 years of India's independence, Congress has ruled our country for more than 53 years, according to a data on January 2020. On 22 May 2004, Manmohan Singh was appointed as the Prime Minister of India following the victory of the Congress & the left front in 2004 Lok Sabha election. The UPA ruled India without any support from the

Left Front. Previously, Atal Bihari Vajpayee had taken office in 1999 after a general election in which BJP-led coalition of 13 parties called the National Democratic Alliance emerged with a huge majority. In May 2014, Narendra Modi of BJP was elected as the Prime Minister of India.

Political Scenario of Other Countries with Respect to India:

The first Country that we will be referring to is none other than the United States of America (USA). The political scenario of the USA is a federal constitution republic where the President, the Congress and the Judiciary share powers with each other which are actually reserved to the national government, and federal powers gradually share sovereignty with the states together. The executive area is taken care by the President, the legislative area is taken care by two chambers of the congress i.e. the Senate and the House of Representatives. The judicial branch is divided into two sub parts i.e. Supreme Court and lower federal courts. The tasks which are looked after by the judiciary are to interpret the Constitution of USA and also the federal laws and regulations. All the layout and hierarchy of the federal government is mentioned under the provisions of the constitution. Unlike the UK and other similar systems of parliament, Americans vote for a specific candidate instead of directly selecting any particular political party.

With a federal government, officials are elected at the federal, state and local levels. Whereas, on a national level, the President is elected indirectly by the people, through an Electoral College. Legal requirements for the candidates who want to stand for presidential elections have remained the same since the year Washington accepted the presidency. As directed by the Constitution, a perfect presidential candidate must be a natural born citizen of the United States, a resident for 14 years, and 35 years of age or older. These requirements do not prohibit women or minority candidates from running.

The next country we are going to discuss is Russia. The system of Russia is under the idea of the Federal Semi Presidential Republic. According to the constitution, the President is the head of the country who looks after all the affairs of the country and also looks after the multi-party system with executive power, headed by the Prime Minister who is appointed by the President by the approval of the parliament. The legislative power is basically vested in the two houses of the Federal Assembly of the Russian Federation. Since the Soviet Union has collapsed, Russia has really faced a lot in gearing up their political system once again and thus they had to follow almost seventy-five years of soviet political governance. Once a new constitution and new government were formed and came into existence, Russia slowly came to a positive stabilisation at their political scenario. The regions of Russia gained political and all other support from Moscow.

At this federal stage, Russia elects a president who is the head of the state and a legislature which is one of the two chambers of the assembly. The president is elected for two consecutive terms of six years by the people. The federal assembly has two branches. The State Duma has around 450 members elected for the term of five years. Since 1990, there have been seven elections for the president and seven for the parliament. The last presidential election was held in the year 2018, and the next is expected to be in 2024. Presidency in the Russian Federation is subjected to the articles 80-93 of the Russian Constitution, the information provided in these articles is explanatory to the system of elections in Russia, and the main points to be highlighted are the following:

- The president is elected on the basis of universal, equal, and direct suffrage through secret ballots.
- The president is to be elected for a term of six years.
- Any citizen of the Russian Federation with 35 or more years of age and that has had a permanent residence for at least 10 years in Russia can run for the presidency in Russia.
- The same person may not be elected President of the Russian Federation for more than two terms running.

Talking about the parliament, there are around 450 seats out of which half of the seats are allocated through proportional representation party voting, with a threshold of around 5%. The legislative body is subjected to articles 94-109 of the Russian Constitution and explain some important points about the elections for the parliament which are as follows:

The Parliament/ State Duma is elected for a proportionate term of five years.

Any Russian Citizen who is at least 21 years old can be a candidate.

The president is to call the elections for the State Duma, according to the provisions in the constitution.

The Federation Council is elected indirectly, appointing one member of the government and one member from the legislative branch for each of 85 federal units of Russia according to the relevant laws and the provisions of the Constitution, as amended.

Politicians of India:

The next thing which we are going to discuss is the Politicians of India. The politicians represent our country or states not only in our country but outside too. From Prime Minister to Chief Ministers, all play a key role in handling the grievances of the common citizens and solve their problems soon. A politician is a person who is highly active in party politics, or a person who basically holds an office of profit under the government.

They use their knowledge and wisdom in framing the laws and regulations i.e. the actual way in which they want to handle their state or area or country as a whole. Precisely speaking a politician can be anyone who seeks to attain political power in any bureaucratic institute. Their posts and positions vary from executive, legislative or judiciary or national governments. They give speeches to people before voting so that they can gain the trust of the people and also if they win, they carry out various activities for the benefit. India has a quite unique system of politics as compared to the other countries. Politics of necessity has become expert users of the media. Earlier in the 19th century, they used the media as a part of their campaign rather than taking out any rally. Once a politician is elected, he/ she becomes the part of the government who has to deal with the permanent bureaucracy of the non-political members.

We have seen that there are various hot heated fights with words among them every time. We have also seen some of them a part of a huge scam or something upon the other. Our country is actually lagging behind in choosing them. The main reason behind this is that we don't have basic guidelines framed for the qualifications that we actually need in a politician. Age and experience do matter but also one more thing which matters is education. If we elect wisely then, the benefit will fall upon us only.

Educational and Other Qualifications Required for Candidates:

Our Constitution does not contain any proper provisions regarding the qualifications that are needed for the Candidates for standing at the elections. Till now we just have simple qualifications i.e. resident of the country or a particular area/state from where he wants to stand, a particular age of majority and not holding any office of profit. We see that there are no such educational and other moral qualifications mentioned for them. We saw that in other countries there are somehow educational qualifications needed even though it is not mentioned. From France to the USA we have quite educated politicians who represent their country and thus the citizens are quite relaxed there.

As per various data and studies we have also seen that many foreign countries perform well at the country's growth and economic patterns and also maintain their social backgrounds. But in India we do not see such changes or any reputable rate of economy and other social factors. Even for crimes or safety of women, various countries have quite stricter rules because of which crimes, rape, assault, dacoity and all other sorts of social evils are less or even not there. If you commit crime at Saudi Arabia, punishments include public beheading, stoning, amputation and lashing. Serious offences not only include internationally recognized crimes but also apostasy, adultery, witchcraft and sorcery. If someone commits a crime in the USA, then that particular person is punished with Capital Punishment. In all sorts of crimes committed, Capital Punishment is imposed. As we talk about the safety of women, Iceland followed by New Zealand and Austria ranks top 3 amongst all the other nations. If we talk about India, it ranks 133 out of 167 countries according to Georgetown University's Institute for Women report. This is the reason why India is lagging behind because there are no set of criteria given. If we impose such things then our country can progress a lot better than other countries.

Now talking about the economy rates, USA, China and Japan ranks in the Top 3 having 21.4%, 14.1% and 5.2% respectively. Looking at all these factors we can only say that India needs to do a lot of hard-work then only we can succeed. Yes, today India is appreciated because of their efforts against Covid-19. India is doing quite well in their fight against this deadly pandemic which has infected millions of people and killed lakhs. The lawmakers need to understand the fact that still we need to have a proper criterion framed for them so that we progress more nicely and, in the end, we don't have to depend upon any other nations for any import-export or any monetary help.

The qualifications that are needed for a candidate is that they should attain at-least 70 percent at their class XII examinations and also, they should be a college graduate with a reputable percentage of marks irrespective of which stream. If that particular candidate has a knowledge of Political Science that will be really good. More emphasis should be given to those who have studied Humanities. The particular candidate should belong from a reputable background and also, he/she should not at all have any crime record. We have seen many political personalities having a huge crime record and also involved in corruption and all other sorts of malpractices which are against the morals of the society.

Therefore, we need candidates who are not involved in all these. Also, the age of a candidate should be such that he/she can handle situations easily and also take proper decisions whenever needed. Most preferably, young candidates should be given a chance because they can actively take part in the decisions and use their knowledge wherever needed. There are certain subjects which play a key role and we used to study since our childhood i.e. Value Education, Moral Science and Basic Science which also plays a key role over here.

Also talking about the background, the candidate should belong from a reputed family as mentioned earlier because family are the ones who teach moral values and proper care and education. Not only bookish knowledge is necessary over here but also knowledge from parents, grandparents and also all the other members of the society. Therefore, these are the only recommendations from my side that are needed so as to get proper politicians who can actually make a huge difference.

Conclusion:

In conclusion, as democratic citizens, we must collectively advocate for reforms in the political system. By demanding qualifications and accountability from our leaders, we can contribute to a more competent and transparent political landscape. Let us work together to strengthen our democracy and ensure that those entrusted with power are truly committed to serving the best interests of the nation and its citizens

The Indian Politics runs within the framework of the Country's Constitution. Our country follows 'Dual Polity System' i.e. A Double Government which consists of Central Authority at the Centre and State at the periphery. Our constitution defines various organizational powers and also certain limitations of both center and state governments which is well organized, rigid and supreme. The actual purpose of an election is to give the people a chance to choose their representatives and make a government of their choice who basically frames policies to address their concerns.

Elections in India take place every 5 years. India has three levels of government- central, state and local. We follow the principle of 'Universal Adult Franchise' which gives rights to every citizen to have one vote and each vote will be treated equally. All the system and procedure of elections are carried out by a separate body known as 'Election Commission' where there are certain members of the office who look after the process in a fair manner. It is ensured that not a single citizen is denied their basic right, we have a system of voters list where the names of the voters are given so that they get to know about it. The voter lists are updated every 5 years.

The principle of free and fair elections is quite important postulate in the branch of democracy, that usually is a part of the Constitution of India. Election system is the only thing through which all the citizens can enjoy their basic rights and also liberties. This system also has a benefit at increasing the morals and also intellectual levels of the citizens. The weakness of this system is actually found in the social, economic or historical factors.

As this system will get damaged or perish or even it may get end but it will never die at all. Also, politicians play a key role in the country's political system. Without them our country cannot progress and thus we will not at all be bound by any law or provision. In the end I would like to conclude my paper by saying that we should choose our leaders wisely and also leaders should use their power correctly and in a proper manner because their decisions are most important for us too.

Politicians should have a proper criterion before elections take place. Therefore, it is the responsibility of the

Election Commission to have a proper set of guidelines and also a way in which they can carry out a smooth process. India has the potential to progress quite well as compared to other countries. Thus, I hope that we have proper qualifications in the coming future and we elect good leaders.

□

Chapter VII

Understanding the Controversial Term "Deshdrohi"

Title: "Deshdrohi (Traitor): Revisiting Democracy and Justice in Independent India"

In this chapter, we embark on a journey to explore the complex and contentious term "Deshdrohi," which has historical roots in India's colonial past. Despite gaining independence in 1947, remnants of the British-imposed Indian Penal Code (IPC) of 1860 continue to influence India's legal landscape. This raises the question of whether a term like "Deshdrohi," historically used to denote actions against society's well-being, can retain relevance in a nation governed by laws inherited from foreign rule.

Analysis of the Farmers' Agitation in 2020:

The year 2020 witnessed a significant farmers' agitation, a protest marked by bravery, conviction, and tragic loss of lives. Unfortunately, some protesters faced convictions under archaic provisions of the IPC as "Deshdrohi." This raise concerns in a democratic India, where freedom of speech and expression is a fundamental right. The criminalization of dissent undermines the very essence of democracy, where citizens should be able to express their views without fear of persecution.

Farms Bill:

The Punjab government data accessed by The Indian Express showed that till July 20, details of 220 such farmers/farm labourers who died in the agitation have been verified. Out of these 220, 203 (92%) farmers/farm labourers deceased were from Malwa region of the state, while 11 (5%) deaths were from Majha and six (2.7%) from Doaba.

The Samyukta Kisan Morcha, the body spearheading the farmer protest, has put the figure to over 670 deaths. A day after Prime Minister Narendra Modi announced the rollback of the farm laws, the farmers' body stated, "So far, more than 670 protesters have sacrificed their lives in this movement. The Modi government has refused to acknowledge the high human cost. The martyrs also deserve homage to be paid to them in the Parliament session, and a memorial erected in their name."

Meanwhile, Congress leader Priyanka Gandhi has claimed that about 700 farmers had lost their lives in the protest. On the first day of the Winter Session of Parliament, the Congress leader had tweeted, "700 farmers were martyred in the farmers' protest. Their martyrdom was not spoken about in Parliament today, nor was it respected by paying tribute."

The Haryana government has registered 136 cases till date against farmers and those protesting against the Centre's three agriculture laws. Only in some cases have the offenders been identified or booked by name, but in majority of such cases, the state has booked thousands of unknown farmers/protesters.

In some districts, police have even booked from 10,000 to 12,000 unknown persons in a single FIR in connection with the farmers protest. The highest number of 26 FIRs have been registered in Sonipat district, in which thousands of persons have been booked, followed by Ambala (15 FIRs) and Kurukshetra (14 FIRs).

The state has also slapped the sedition charge in two such cases. One such case was registered in Sirsa on July 11 against three identified and 80-90 other persons for attacking the vehicle of deputy speaker of Haryana assembly Ranbir Singh Gangwa during his visit there. The other case was registered on January 15 at police station Bahadurgarh against Sunil Gulia who had uploaded a video on social media in which he vowed to launch a cannon attack against the government, if it did not listen to the protesting farmers. (Times Of India)

The APMCs:

Agricultural Produce Market Committees (APMC) are marketing organizations set up by state governments to stop farmers from being exploited by middlemen and compelled to sell their produce at extortionate prices. Additionally, APMCs are actual marketplaces with auctions for sales that are designed to ensure fair prices and prompt payment of farmers for their produce.

Because of this, only 7000 of the 42,000 mandies (markets) needed for our size nation really exist. Because they cannot transport their produce to faraway mandis, farmers frequently wind up selling their produce to private individuals while also paying the mandi charge. Within five kilometres of their communities, well-run mandis offer farmers guaranteed procurement prices.

Overriding the current APMCs won't do anything but produce a parallel market. Its rules are entirely different. Traders in APMCs will need licenses and payment. Grant the government access to valuable intelligence. Like private sponsors, the state's capacity to control the produce trade will be weakened. The mandis will also fall apart.

The farmers, who are the real stakeholders, will not be consulted during the creation of these Acts. Farmers are not given fixed pricing (MSP) or player monitoring by them. Likewise, market regulation by the state government is not made possible by transactions or prices.

Government Charges Against Farmers:

The government's response to the farmers' protests was varied, with charges filed under different legal provisions. The use of Section 124A of the IPC, which deals with sedition, against certain individuals alleged incitement of violence and contempt towards the government. Additionally, charges of conspiracy and unlawful activities were levelled against activists and organizations associated with the protests. The indiscriminate use of the term "Deshdrohi" against those who expressed dissent, even on Independence Day, is indicative of the sensitivity surrounding this term.

Constitutional Provisions Applicable to Farmer's Protests:

India's Constitution enshrines fundamental rights that are fundamental to democracy. These rights include freedom of speech and expression, the right to peaceful assembly, and the right to freedom of movement. Additionally, Article 14 guarantees equality before the law and protection of the laws, while Directive Principles of State Policy emphasize fair treatment and well-being for farmers. These constitutional provisions must serve as guiding principles when dealing with protests and dissent.

The Need to Amend the IPC:

As India progresses as a democratic nation, the IPC's colonial vestiges demand reconsideration. The legal system should evolve in line with constitutional principles and changing times. Pre-independence precedents should be revisited, and judgments reevaluated to align with contemporary democratic values. A nation that cherishes freedom must dispense justice that reflects the spirit of the Constitution.

Supreme Court of India involvement:

The Supreme Court of India has received numerous petitions seeking direction to remove protesting farmers from blocking access routes to the capital. The Supreme Court has also conveyed to the central government that it intends to set up a body for taking forward the negotiations. On 17 December, the Supreme Court acknowledged the right to peaceful protest but added, "you (farmers) have a purpose also and that purpose is served only if you talk, discuss and reach a conclusion". The central government opposed the court's recommendation of putting on hold the implementation of the farm laws. Agitating farmer unions have decided to consult Prashant Bhushan, Dushyant Dave, HS Phoolka and Colin Gonsalves as far as the Supreme Court proceedings go.

A plea submitted by several students of Panjab University on 2 December 2020 was registered by the Supreme Court as a public petition on 4 January 2021. The plea was in the form of a letter which called out police excesses, illegal detentions of protesters, "misrepresentation, polarization and sensationalisation" by media channels and approached the matter on humanitarian grounds. A student who drafted the petition informed The Wire that "over the course of over 100 days of the farmers' protest, this is the first petition filed in favour of the protest".

Farmers have said they will not listen to the courts if told to back off or even if the laws are stayed. Farmer union leaders have also raised the issue of the government "dodging dialogue" since the "SC has said earlier that it will not intervene". Congress chief spokesperson Randeep Surjewala made a statement in this regard, "Why does the government want the SC to solve all contentious issues, from the CAA and the National Register of Citizens to farm laws?"

On 11 January 2021 the Chief Justice of India said during hearings, "We are not experts on agriculture and economics. Tell us whether you (the government) will put these laws on hold or else we will do it. What's the prestige issue here? [...] We don't know if you are part of the solution or part of the problem [...] We have an apprehension that someday maybe, there might be a breach of peace. Each one of us will be responsible if anything goes wrong [...] If the vast majority says that laws are good, let them say it to (a) committee." The Court also stated to the government that they were "...extremely disappointed at the way government is handling all this (farmers protests). We don't know what consultative process you followed before the laws. Many states are up in rebellion." The Court also rejected a claim by Solicitor General Tushar Mehta that the "vast majority" of farmers supported the laws, stating that they had not received any submissions from any person that the laws were beneficial.

Supreme Court stay order and farm laws committee:

On 12 January 2021, the Supreme Court of India suspended the farm laws and formed a committee to look into the grievances of protesting farmers. The CJI, Sharad Arvind Bobde, requested the farmer unions to cooperate. The members of the committee included agriculture experts Ashok Gulati, Pramod Kumar Joshi, Anil Ghanwat and Bhupinder Singh Mann. However, two days later, Bhupinder Singh Mann recused himself in solidarity with the farmers.

Irrespective of Mann recusing himself, and the following criticism, the Supreme Court, and the remaining members of the Supreme Court-appointed committee, continued with the tasks outlined to the committee. Criticism raised, related to bias in appointing the committee, was addressed by the Supreme Court. The committee called on the public for suggestions by 20 February 2021. It went on to conduct a number of meetings online, including speaking to 73 farmers organisations and related organisations.

The report was submitted to the Supreme Court on 19 March 2021. Committee members requested the report be made public three times. Following the repeal of the laws the report was released by committee member Anil Ghanwat on 21 March 2022.

Conclusion:

This chapter delves into the complexities surrounding the term "Deshdrohi" and its connection to India's history, laws, and democracy. As India marches towards a future characterized by democracy and justice, the legal framework must uphold the values of liberty, equality, and free expression. Criminalizing dissent and misusing archaic laws to stifle voices undermine the spirit of democracy.

To forge a just and progressive society, it is essential to confront the past, challenge prevailing norms, and carve a path that embodies the true essence of democratic India. Only then can the nation ensure that justice prevails, and citizens' rights are protected, ushering in a brighter and more equitable future for all. Embracing democratic principles and safeguarding the right to dissent are crucial steps towards this endeavour.

□

Chapter VIII

Balancing VIP Privileges and Public Welfare

Title: "VIP Privileges and Public Perception: Balancing Security and Equality"

Preferential treatments for VIPs and their relatives, such as exemptions from certain rules, VIP queues, and special treatment, are practices observed in several countries. The intention behind such provisions is to ensure the safety and security of high-ranking government officials and foreign dignitaries. However, it is essential to strike a balance between providing security and privileges to VIPs and ensuring the welfare and equality of the general public.

Disruption of Normal Life: While providing security and streamlined movement to VIPs is crucial, it should not come at the cost of disrupting normal life or causing chaos in traffic. Authorities responsible for VIP movements should strive to minimize disruptions and ensure that public life is not severely impacted while maintaining the safety of the VIPs.

Politicians Acting Responsibly: Public servants, including politicians, are expected to act responsibly and in the best interests of the public. They should not misuse their positions or privileges for personal gain or to inconvenience others. VIP treatments should be governed by legitimate security concerns and not whims and fancies.

VIP Road Blocking: VIP road blocking is a contentious issue in various countries. While there may be valid reasons for such measures, they should be carried out judiciously, and alternative arrangements should be made to minimize public inconvenience.

Cultural and Contextual Factors: Perceptions of VIP treatment can vary based on cultural, historical, and political contexts. Practices that might be acceptable in one country might not be well-received in another. It is essential to be mindful of these cultural sensitivities and ensure that VIP privileges are not abused.

India's Perspective: In India, there is no specific law that entitles the family members of judges or judicial magistrates to use VIP sirens or receive preferential treatment in airports or queues. VIP sirens are reserved for specific government officials and emergency services vehicles for public safety. Airport privileges are typically applied uniformly to all passengers.

Misuse of Authority: Instances of individuals misusing their positions or claiming unwarranted privileges should be treated as misconduct or abuse of power. Such actions should be addressed promptly and held accountable under existing laws. The issue of VIP treatment, both in temples and during travel, has been a cause of frustration among the public. The recent directions issued by the Madras High Court regarding special darshan at a well-known shrine in Tamil Nadu reflect the need to balance special privileges while upholding the principle of equality.

The court emphasized that special darshan should be reserved for individuals holding special offices, not for individuals themselves. VIP entry should only be allowed for VIPs and their immediate family members, excluding relatives. The court firmly stated that God alone is VIP and any inconvenience caused by VIPs to public devotees is considered a religious sin.

The incident involving the President of India's travel, which led to the blockade of Railway Overbridges and a fatal delay for an ambulance, highlights the severe consequences of VIP movement on common people. Thousands of individuals have faced disruptions in their daily lives, but their stories often go unnoticed and unheard.

A 50-year-old woman with post-Covid complications passed away while allegedly stuck in traffic for nearly two hours due to road blockades set up for President. She was on her way to the hospital in Kanpur.

The Kanpur Police Commissionerate declared that the event was "a big lesson for the future" and asked for "forgiveness." It said in a tweet from its official account that the President had "expressed distress" about the passing.

The Indian Industries Association (IIA) Kanpur chapter chairwoman, Vandana Mishra, was headed to a private hospital when her vehicle got stuck in traffic between the Govindpuri flyover and the Nand Lal intersection.

"The President's visit to Kanpur caused heavy traffic and the closure of several roads." We normally need twenty to thirty minutes to travel the distance to the hospital, but it took us almost two hours. Her husband, Sharad Mishra (58), stated, "We were unable to get through the traffic jam despite some police officers' attempts to assist us and allow our vehicle to pass.

He said, "When we got to the hospital, the doctors declared her dead and said she could have been saved if we had brought her in 20 minutes earlier."

"Honourable President expressed distress over the

untimely death of Vandana Mishra," the Kanpur Police Commissionerate tweeted. Inquiring about the incident and expressing his grief, he called the District Magistrate and the Commissioner of Kanpur Police. He gave the officials instructions to make sure the family receives his message.

"Both the Kanpur City Police and me personally ask for your pardon. We can learn a lot from this for the future. The Kanpur Police Commissionerate tweeted, "We promise to make sure that our route arrangement is such that citizens have to wait for the least amount of time so that such incidents are not repeated."

The commissioner of Kanpur Police, announced that four officers had been suspended for delaying traffic beyond the designated time. "Citizens should not experience security-related issues, particularly in the event of medical emergencies. In a statement, he said, "We are improving procedures to ensure that such an incident does not occur again.

The incident is being looked into, according to B B G T S Murthy, the deputy commissioner of police (traffic) for Kanpur.

According to a police officer, the movement of VIPs had blocked several roads. In the city to greet the President were the Chief Minister and the Governor. According to him, one of the routes that had to be blocked as part of the security protocol was the one on which Mishra's car got stuck.

sadly there have been other incidents where sick people have perished as a result of being stuck in traffic because of VIP movements.

Examples of similar cases from the past:

(1) Due to travel restrictions, many people suffered during the nation's lockdown, primarily the impoverished. But thanks to her powerful

father's special permission from the authorities to visit Kota and bring her back, the daughter of a BJP MLA from Bihar who was studying there could safely return, according to the Print.

(2) A bench of the Madras High Court stated in March of this year that people are "frustrated" with the VIP culture, particularly in temples. On Wednesday, the court issued a number of orders pertaining to special darshan at a well-known shrine in Tamil Nadu. During a case hearing concerning the renowned Arulmigu Subramania Swamy Temple in Tiruchendur, Tuticorin district, Justice S M Subramaniam stated that VIP admission should only be granted to themselves and their family members, not to relatives.

"There is no denying that certain individuals are deserving of special darshan. However, these privileges are not extended to the individuals themselves; rather, they are limited to the particular positions that the individuals hold. Only a select few, namely constitutional dignitaries, are protected by the state in the majority of developed nations; the remainder rely on the state to manage its security. The judge stated, "God alone is the VIP. Certain special privileges shall not come in the way of the equality of the citizens."

(3) The Tribune reported that VIP culture is still very much in place at the Chandigarh railway station. The station's main entrance now has a dedicated VIP lane that narrows the width of the adjacent lane for public use and prohibits private vehicles from entering. The Government Railway Police state that the VIP designated lane is meant to protect both the VIPs' safety and the efficient flow of traffic at the station's main entrance.

(4) East Delhi resident Kailash Chand suffered a heart attack in 2016. According to the Hindustan Times, Arvind, his son, tried to take him to the hospital but was stopped by police close to Geeta Colony Pul, which had been closed and traffic diverted. As time went on, Arvind begged the security guards to let him go, but they refused. After that, Chand's autorickshaw made its way through ITO and Mori Gate, stopping at a number of lights before reaching the hospital. The hospital at Lok Nayak is only ten minutes away, but it took them an hour and a half to get there. While traveling, Chand passed away. As part of the Independence Day dress rehearsal, the police informed Arvind that there was "a lot of VVIP movement" in the area and that they couldn't let them through.

(5) Outrage erupted in 2017 when a video of an ambulance in the Central District region stopping for a short while to tend to a bleeding child went viral and was banned from being used for VIP transit. A child was shown on a stretcher in an ambulance during a traffic jam, and some bystanders were attempting to convince police officers to allow the ambulance to pass. The video went viral on social media. In the two-minute video, people are heard declaring that a child's life is more significant than a VIP's itinerary. The incident happened outside gate 14 of the Indira Gandhi Indoor Stadium, which is close to IP Estate. Police claim that because Malaysia's chief of state was scheduled to travel through the route, it was closed to the general public.

Police claimed their officers followed protocol in the wake of the outcry. As stated by MS Randhawa,

Deputy Commissioner of Police (Central), it required several minutes for the police to allow the ambulance to pass. According to him, police officers also escorted the ambulance from the rear of the traffic to the barricade.

(6) When the then-prime minister's route was being sanitized in 2010, a patient passed away while being driven to a hospital. After becoming stuck while the prime minister's path was being cleaned, the patient passed away in an ambulance. The victim, Anil Jain, had reported experiencing chest pain on Sunday afternoon. When Jain's relatives brought him to Guru Tegh Bahadur Hospital, there was no pacemaker on hand to treat him. After that, Jain's relatives continued on to GB Pant Hospital, but they were halted by Singh's motorcade as it was passing by Rajghat. They said they called the 100 police emergency number, but they didn't get any help. The ambulance could not move until PM Singh's cavalcade had passed. But by then, Jain was too late. While traveling to the hospital in the ambulance, he passed away.

(7) People were incensed earlier this month when officials requested that people adjust their travel schedules one day ahead of schedule because of VIP movements in Bengaluru. The North Deputy Commissioner (DCP) tweeted, "Commuters traveling to and from Kempegowda International Airport on Tuesday, May 3, between 11.30 a.m. and 1.30 p.m. are urged to adjust their travel plans owing to traffic congestion caused by dignitaries' movement." It also added a polite request for cooperation from the public. On social media, the public's response to the advice

was harsh; some referred to it as "VIP culture," while others questioned how they could change their travel plans so quickly.

(8) An ambulance transporting a chronic patient was delayed in traffic at Masab Tank junction in July of last year for an extended period of time because Hyderabad Traffic Police stopped cars to allow a Minister's convoy to pass. A video of an ambulance with its siren going off and one of its medical personnel going up to the traffic constable in person, followed by an argument between them, went viral on social media. Netizens questioned the Traffic Police on Twitter and other social media platforms for preventing the medical emergency vehicle from passing the signal when traffic was stopped for the VIP movement, according to the Indian Express.

(9) In 2017, when police blocked traffic on Queen's Road in Bengaluru to allow the convoy of then-Home Minister G Parameshwara to pass, an ambulance was stopped for nearly fifteen minutes. Following a meeting at the Karnataka Pradesh Congress Committee (KPCC) office, traffic policemen blocked Queen's Road so that G Parameshwara's convoy could pass. Meanwhile, traffic caused an ambulance headed to Bhagwan Mahaveer Jain Hospital to come to a stop. According to the Deccan Herald, a 60-year-old patient who had suffered a heart attack was being transported by ambulance from a private hospital.

(10) In a recent report, TBS stated that a schoolboy passed away in the ambulance while traveling to the hospital in Kathalbari Ferry Ghat, Madaripur,

as a result of a three-hour wait for a ministry joint secretary on the ferry.

The courts have consistently expressed concern over this issue, deprecating the practice of inconveniencing the common man due to VIP movement. The judicial system aims to strike a balance between ensuring VIP security and safeguarding the constitutional rights of citizens.

Also, addressing the VIP treatment issue requires careful consideration to avoid infringing upon the rights and well-being of the public. The courts' efforts to find a fair approach are commendable, and it remains crucial to implement measures that respect both VIP security concerns and the equality of citizens.

Conclusion:

Balancing VIP privileges and public welfare is an ongoing challenge for governments worldwide. While providing security to VIPs is necessary, it should not infringe upon the rights and equality of the public. The principles of fairness, transparency, and accountability must guide decisions related to VIP treatment. By upholding these values, societies can ensure that VIP privileges serve their intended purpose while maintaining a level playing field for all citizens. As we move forward, it is essential to evolve our practices and policies to foster a more inclusive and just society for everyone.

While the current government in India has made commendable efforts to control public chaos by restricting VIP sirens and lights, there is a pressing need for additional measures in remote cities. Despite these regulations, the issue persists in certain areas, where VIP movements continue to bring everything to a standstill. To address this, a comprehensive approach is required, focusing on enhancing traffic management systems and ensuring the equitable enforcement of regulations across all regions. Implementing these measures in remote cities would contribute significantly to alleviating traffic issues and promoting a more streamlined and efficient transportation system nationwide.

□

Chapter IX

Understanding Legal Insurance and Its Benefits

Title: "The Growing Need for Legal Insurance: Empowering Society and Promoting Justice"

Legal insurance, a concept not widely prevalent in India until recently, has gained recognition as a valuable tool for empowering individuals and promoting justice in society. This chapter explores the meaning of legal insurance and its numerous benefits that can have a significant impact on the weaker sections of society and the overall legal landscape.

What is Legal Insurance?

Legal insurance is a type of insurance that provides coverage for legal expenses when individuals require legal representation or assistance. It aims to make legal services more accessible by alleviating the burden of high costs that can often hinder people from seeking legal remedies. Depending on the policy's terms, legal insurance can cover a range of legal matters, including civil cases, family disputes, property issues, and criminal defence.

Legal insurance, also known as prepaid legal or group legal, offers coverage that grants individuals and families access to a network of qualified attorneys. With legal insurance, participants can receive advice, have attorneys review and draft legal documents, and receive consultation or representation in court.

Benefits Of Legal Insurance In India:

Legal insurance can potentially provide several benefits to India, particularly in terms of increasing access to justice and promoting legal awareness.

Firstly, legal insurance can help to bridge the gap between those who can afford legal representation and those who cannot. Many people in India, particularly those from disadvantaged backgrounds, may not have access to affordable legal services. Legal insurance can help to provide financial support for legal expenses and increase access to legal representation, which can help to ensure that everyone has equal access to justice.

Secondly, legal insurance can help to promote legal awareness and education in India. Many people may not be aware of their legal rights or the legal procedures involved in resolving disputes. By providing access to legal representation, legal insurance can help to educate people about their legal rights and responsibilities, which can lead to better decision-making and improved outcomes in legal disputes.

Thirdly, legal insurance can help to reduce the burden on the Indian judicial system. With a large population and a significant backlog of cases, the Indian judicial system is often overburdened and slow to provide justice. Legal insurance can help to resolve disputes quickly and efficiently, reducing the strain on the judicial system and freeing up resources for more complex cases.

Legal insurance can potentially provide several benefits to India, including increased access to justice, legal awareness and education, and reduced burden on the judicial system. However, it is important to note that the success of legal insurance in India will depend on factors such as the availability and affordability of insurance policies, the quality of legal representation provided, and the effectiveness of the judicial system in resolving disputes.

Benefits of Legal Insurance:

Legal insurance is often misunderstood, with many people assuming it's only relevant for individuals involved in criminal cases. However, legal insurance, provides coverage for various personal legal matters, including labor disputes, marital matters, civil cases, and legal document assistance.

Affordability: Legal expenses can be daunting for many, especially those with limited financial means. Legal insurance bridges this gap, making legal services more affordable and accessible to a broader section of society.

Legal Awareness: By offering legal insurance, there is an opportunity to increase legal awareness among the general population. Policyholders may become more informed about their rights and the available legal options, empowering them to make informed decisions.

Reduced Burden on the Legal System: Legal insurance can help alleviate the burden on the already overburdened legal system by promoting early dispute resolution through mediation or arbitration. This, in turn, can expedite the resolution of cases and reduce the backlog in courts.

Protection against Unforeseen Legal Issues: Just as health insurance safeguards against unexpected health problems, legal insurance provides protection against unforeseen legal issues that may arise in personal or professional life.

Access to Quality Legal Representation: Legal insurance ensures that policyholders have access to competent legal professionals, promoting a fair and just representation in legal matters.

Peace of Mind: Legal insurance for individuals provides peace of mind by ensuring they have access to professional legal advice and support whenever they need it. For example, imagine being involved in a motor vehicle accident and facing a complex insurance claim. With legal insurance, you can consult with an experienced lawyer who will guide you through the process, ensuring that your rights are protected and increasing the chances of a favorable outcome.

Financial Protection: Legal expenses can quickly escalate, placing a significant burden on individuals. With legal insurance, such as the coverage provided by Alliance Legal, you gain financial protection against these costs. Let's say you find yourself in an unexpected employment dispute with your company. Legal insurance would cover the costs of hiring a lawyer to represent you, saving you from bearing the full financial burden and allowing you to focus on resolving the issue.

Coverage for Labor Matters: Workplace disputes and employment-related issues can arise at any time. Legal insurance can help individuals facing labor matters, such as unfair dismissals, workplace discrimination, or wage disputes. For instance, if you believe you have been wrongfully terminated, legal insurance would cover the legal fees associated with filing a claim against your employer, ensuring that you have the resources to fight for your rights.

Support for Marital Matters: Marital issues, such as divorce or child custody disputes, can be emotionally and financially draining. Legal insurance can provide coverage for such matters, ensuring that you have the legal support you need during these challenging times. Consider a situation where you are going through a divorce and need assistance with child custody arrangements. Legal insurance would cover the fees for a family lawyer who can help you navigate the legal complexities and protect your interests.

Assistance with Civil Matters: Legal insurance also extends to civil matters, such as property disputes, contract disagreements, or personal injury claims. Having coverage in these areas allows individuals to pursue legal action, defend their rights, and seek fair compensation without incurring substantial legal expenses. For example, if you are involved in a contract dispute with a vendor, legal insurance would cover the costs of legal representation to help resolve the issue and protect your business interests.

Help with Legal Documents: Navigating legal documents can be complex and confusing. Legal insurance often includes services to assist with the preparation and review of legal documents, such as contracts, wills, or powers of attorney. Let's say you're starting a business and need assistance drafting a contract. Legal insurance would provide access to legal professionals who can ensure the contract is comprehensive, legally binding, and tailored to your specific needs.

Legal Insurance and the Weaker Sections of Society: The weaker sections of society, often comprising marginalized communities and individuals with limited resources, face a higher vulnerability when it comes to legal matters. Legal issues like land disputes, domestic violence, labor rights violations, and discrimination are prevalent in these communities.

Legal insurance can significantly benefit the weaker sections by:

Empowerment: Legal insurance empowers individuals from marginalized backgrounds to seek legal recourse without the fear of financial burden. It instils confidence in standing up for their rights.

Enhanced Access to Justice: By providing affordable legal services, legal insurance ensures improved access to justice for those who may otherwise struggle to afford legal representation.

Preventive Measures: Legal insurance can encourage preventive legal action and early dispute resolution, preventing conflicts from escalating and protecting vulnerable individuals from prolonged legal battles.

Protection of Rights: Many weaker sections face systemic injustices and violations of their rights. Legal insurance can aid in safeguarding and upholding their rights.

Importance of Legal Help for Every Citizen: Access to legal assistance is crucial for every citizen to ensure.

Upholding the Rule of Law: Legal help ensures that the rule of law is upheld, promoting a just and fair society where no one is above the law.

Protection of Rights: Legal help empowers citizens to protect their rights in matters such as property, employment, healthcare, and other legal issues.

Dispute Resolution: Legal assistance is essential for the peaceful and lawful resolution of disputes between individuals, businesses, or organizations.

Ensuring Justice: Access to legal help ensures that individuals receive fair treatment and representation in courts and legal proceedings.

How Legal Insurance Can Help Society and

Minimize Crimes: Legal insurance can contribute to a safer and more just society by:

Acting as a Crime Deterrent: Legal insurance can discourage potential wrongdoers, knowing that their victims have access to legal assistance, increasing the chances of bringing them to justice.

Promoting Efficient Dispute Resolution: By making legal services accessible, legal insurance facilitates efficient dispute resolution, preventing conflicts from escalating into criminal activities.

Promoting Legal Compliance: Legal insurance can educate individuals about their legal responsibilities and rights, leading to increased compliance with the law and reduced criminal activities.

Supporting Crime Victims: Legal insurance can offer support to victims of crimes, helping them navigate the legal process and seek appropriate compensation or justice.

Strengthening the Legal System: By reducing the burden on the legal system and promoting early dispute resolution, legal insurance contributes to a more efficient and effective legal system, ensuring justice is served promptly.

Scope of Legal Insurance In The Development of Economy:

Civil litigation: This can include legal expenses related to disputes over contracts, property, or other civil matters.

Employment law: Legal insurance may cover expenses related to disputes between employers and employees, such as wrongful termination or discrimination claims.

Criminal defense: Some legal insurance policies may provide coverage for legal expenses related to criminal charges or investigations.

Family law: Legal insurance may also cover expenses

related to divorce, child custody, or other family law matters.

Identity theft and fraud: Some legal insurance policies may provide coverage for legal expenses related to identity theft, fraud, or other types of financial crime.

The Scope of Legal Insurance Can Have A Positive Impact on The Development of The Economy of A Country In Several Ways:

Firstly, it can provide individuals and businesses with greater access to legal services. This can help to level the playing field and ensure that justice is served, which can foster a more fair and equitable society. This, in turn, can support economic growth by promoting trust and stability, as investors and entrepreneurs are more likely to invest in a country where the legal system is perceived to be fair and accessible.

Secondly, legal insurance can help to reduce the risk of costly legal disputes and litigation. This can be particularly important for small businesses and individuals, who may not have the resources to absorb the financial impact of a major legal battle. By providing coverage for legal expenses, legal insurance can help to mitigate the risk of financial hardship resulting from legal disputes, which can encourage greater entrepreneurship and investment.

Thirdly, legal insurance can help to promote compliance with the law. By providing coverage for legal expenses, legal insurance can encourage individuals and businesses to seek legal advice and guidance, which can help them to avoid legal disputes and comply with the law. This can reduce the burden on the legal system, freeing up resources that can be used to support economic development.

The availability of legal insurance can help to support a healthy and vibrant economy by promoting access to justice, reducing legal risks, and fostering greater economic stability and growth. By providing greater access to legal services and mitigating the financial impact of legal disputes, legal insurance can help to create a more fair and equitable society, which can in turn support greater investment, entrepreneurship, and economic growth.

How The Indian Economy Will Be Benefited By Legal Insurance:

Legal insurance can potentially provide several benefits to the Indian economy, particularly in terms of promoting business growth and reducing the cost of doing business.

Firstly, legal insurance can help to promote business growth by providing financial support for legal expenses. Many businesses in India may face legal issues such as contract disputes, intellectual property infringements, or regulatory compliance issues. Legal insurance can provide businesses with the financial support they need to defend themselves against legal claims and protect their assets, which can help to promote business growth and innovation.

Secondly, legal insurance can help to reduce the cost of doing business in India. Legal expenses can be a significant financial burden for businesses, particularly small and medium-sized enterprises (SMEs). Legal insurance can help to reduce the cost of legal expenses and provide businesses with a more predictable and manageable legal budget, which can help to reduce the cost of doing business and improve their competitiveness.

Thirdly, legal insurance can help to improve the legal infrastructure in India. By promoting legal awareness and education and increasing access to justice, legal insurance can help to build a stronger and more efficient legal system in India. This can help to improve the overall business environment and attract more investment to the country.

Legal insurance can potentially provide several benefits to the Indian economy, including promoting business growth, reducing the cost of doing business, and improving the legal infrastructure. However, it is important to note that the success of legal insurance in India will depend on factors such as the availability and affordability of insurance policies, the quality of legal representation provided, and the effectiveness of the judicial system in resolving disputes.

Impact of Legal Insurance In The Development of Indian Economy:

Insurance is a big deal not just in the world of business but also contributes to the economy as a whole. It has a huge impact on how businesses evolve, how people think about economics and how the world moves forward. Insurance is the bedrock of the economy, and while it may not be something you love, it is something you need to support your business.

The insurance industry is one of the major players in the economy and contributes to the world's economy. This is because they help in the smooth running of the world's economy through the payment of insurance claims and are considered one of the safest investments for people to have.

In a variety of ways, insurance companies contribute to the strength and vitality of our economy.

Conclusion:

The growing need for legal insurance in India holds the potential to empower individuals and ensure access to justice for all sections of society. By providing affordable legal services, promoting legal awareness, and easing the burden on the legal system, legal insurance can foster a fair and just society where every citizen can protect their rights and seek redressal for legal issues. The integration of legal insurance into the country's legal landscape can pave the way for a more inclusive and equitable society, where the weaker sections are empowered, and justice is accessible to all.

Legal insurance, such as that offered by Alliance Legal in Lesotho, provides individuals with a range of benefits. It covers various personal legal matters, including labor disputes, marital matters, civil cases, and legal document assistance. With legal insurance, individuals gain peace of mind, knowing that they have access to quality legal services and financial protection when facing legal challenges. So, whether you're dealing with a labor dispute, marital issue, civil matter, or need assistance with legal documents, legal insurance can be a valuable investment in safeguarding your rights and interests.

□

Chapter X

Redefining the Paradigm of Reservation

Title: "Equity and Meritocracy: Reforming Reservation in India"

In this pivotal chapter, we delve deep into the contentious issue of reservation in India, exploring its impact on the education system and the lives of students. While the noble intent behind reservation was to uplift marginalized communities, its implementation has given rise to unforeseen challenges that demand urgent attention.

Reservation in the Constitution of India:

The reservation is mentioned in Article 46 of Part IV of the Constitution of India, which contains Directive Principles of State Policy (DPSPs). These provisions are non-enforceable but are meant to serve as guiding principles for lawmakers. Several of the provisions mentioned here, including reservations, have been made into laws over the years.

"Since 1950, the successive governments at the Centre and in the states have made several laws and formulated various programmes for implementing the Directive Principles of State Policies," notes M. Laxmikanth in his book Indian Polity, and lists some examples like the establishment of Planning Commission, laws for minimum wages and equal treatment of workers, maternity benefit laws, legal aid provisions, etc.

Article 46 states, "The state shall promote with special care the educational and economic interests of the weaker sections of the people, and, in particular, of the Scheduled Castes and the Scheduled Tribes, and shall protect them from social injustice and all forms of exploitation."

The principle of Article 46 is reflected in Articles 15 and 16 of the Constitution which actually provide for the provisions of reservations in education and employment.

Moreover, Articles 330 and 332 of the Constitution reserve seats for SCs and STs in Lok Sabha and state assemblies.

However, the provisions in Article 15 were only added in 1951 through a constitutional amendment after the Supreme Court judgement nullified state reservations.

The Conundrum of Merit and Mediocrity:

In the pursuit of equality, the reservation system has unintentionally generated a paradox: the struggle between meritorious students who toil diligently and those benefiting from reservation without demonstrating the same level of academic prowess. This lopsided competition has led to an unhealthy educational environment, wherein the true value of merit is compromised.

Unmasking the Tragic Outcomes:

The consequences of this imbalanced system are nothing short of tragic. Cutthroat competition ensues for the limited reserved seats, fostering an atmosphere of desperation and anxiety among students. The rampant corruption surrounding these seats further exacerbates the predicament, undermining the integrity of the education system.

The Shadow of Despair: Rising Suicides:

Perhaps the most heart-wrenching aspect of this issue is the rising toll on students' mental health. The undue pressure to secure a place in coveted institutions, coupled with the fear of losing out due to reservation, has resulted in an alarming increase in student suicides. This dark reality impels us to question the status quo and advocate for much-needed reforms.

The Call for Judicial Intervention:

While the reservation system was initiated with good intentions, its execution warrants a critical revaluation. As we delve into this chapter, we implore the judiciary to take a proactive role in reassessing the percentage of reservation, aiming to strike a balance that truly upholds both equity and meritocracy.

A Path Towards Holistic Reform:

This chapter does not seek to undermine the importance of social justice but rather to explore avenues that align with the principles of merit-based education. By drawing insights from global models and engaging in constructive dialogue, we hope to chart a path that empowers all students to achieve their potential, irrespective of their backgrounds.

Ultimately, the question before us is this: Can we envision a future where a more refined, equitable, and inclusive system replaces the current reservation model? In this pursuit, we must navigate a delicate balance between acknowledging historical injustices and nurturing an environment that fosters genuine merit and excellence.

Supreme Court judgements on reservation:

Reservation policies have seen multiple judicial

interpretations over the years. The first in the series of rulings came soon after the Constitution came into being. The ruling led to the then-Prime Minister Pandit Jawaharlal Nehru to bring a constitutional amendment to overrule it.

Champakam Dorairaj vs State of Madras, 1951:

The Supreme Court ruled that reservations for communities violated the equality provisions in the Constitution of India. The case concerned the reservation province in Madras (present-day Tamil Nadu).

"The classification in the Communal GO [government order, which gave the reservation under dispute in court] proceeds on the basis of religion, race and caste. In our view, the classification made in the Communal GO is opposed to the Constitution and constitutes a clear violation of the fundamental rights guaranteed to the citizen under article 29(2)," said the Supreme Court in its judgement.

To restore caste-based judgement, Nehru brought in the 1st Amendment to the Constitution which enabled reservations by adding Article 15 (4).

"It is laid down in article 46 as a directive principle of state policy that the state should promote with special care the educational and economic interests of the weaker sections of the people and protect them from social injustice. In order that any special provision that the state may make for the educational, economic or social advancement of any backward class of citizens may not be challenged on the ground of being discriminatory, it is proposed that Article 15(3) should be suitably amplified," said Nehru while moving the amendment.

The amendment restored the reservation but had far-reaching consequences as it set precedent for the Executive nullifying court rulings through legislation.

MR Balaji vs State of Mysore, 1963

The Supreme Court judgement introduced the concept of "reasonable limits" on the reservation. It also held that while Article 15 (4) serves the historically disadvantaged, it cannot bypass the interests of the society.

The case was centred around the then-state of Mysore's policy of providing 68 per cent reservation in educational institutions.

The SC said, "Reservation should and must be adopted to advance the prospects of weaker sections of society, but while doing so, care should be taken not to exclude admission to higher educational centres of deserving and qualified candidates of other communities. Reservations under Arts. 15 (4) and 16 (4) must be within reasonable limits.

"The interests of weaker sections of society, which are a first charge on the states and the Centre, have to be adjusted with the interests of the community as a whole. Speaking generally and in a broad way, a special provision should be less than 50 per cent. The actual percentage must depend upon the relevant prevailing circumstances in each case."

This judgement is crucial as it served as the basis of the 50 per cent cap on reservation.

Indra Sawhney vs Union of India, 1992

This is the most well-known judgement on reservation that was pronounced by the Supreme Court. It was in response to a petition filed by Indra Sawhney against the Other Backward Classes (OBC) reservations provided by the government in response to Mandal Commission recommendations.

The Mandal Commission in 1980 recommended 27 per cent reservation to OBCs. The Vishwanath Pratap Singh-led

Union government in 1990 accepted the recommendations. The government decision was challenged and it came up before the nine-judge-bench of the Supreme Court. In all its history, the Supreme Court has had a nine-judge-bench only in 17 cases.

The Supreme Court in a 6:3 judgement upheld the OBC reservation but imposed some conditions. Among other rulings in the case, the Supreme Court gave an important interpretation that reservation is meant to be adequate to disadvantaged communities, not proportional.

"The Apex Court has held that it is not possible to accept the theory of proportionate representation though the proportion of population of Backward Classes to the total population would certainly be relevant and held that the power conferred by clause (4) of article 16 should be exercised in a fair manner and within reasonable limits so that reservation does not exceed 50%," notes a Union government circular as saying of the SC judgement.

The Supreme Court further introduced the concepts of "creamy layer" and reinstated the 50 per cent reservation ceiling. The creamy layer refers to the well-off sections within OBCs. The SC said that such people will be excluded from reservation.

"There are sections among the backward classes who are highly advanced, socially and educationally and they constitute the forward section of that community. These advanced sections do not belong to the true backward class. They are as forward as any other forward class member. If some of the members are far too advanced socially (which in the context necessarily means economically and may also mean educationally), the connecting thread between them and the remaining class snaps," notes the SC in the judgement, as per the copy available on the website.

However, the SC also noted in the judgement that

economic criteria cannot be the only basis for reservation. This part of the Indra Sawhney judgement is central to the criticism and questioning of EWS reservation.

Reservation in India	
Category	**Reservation Percentage**
Scheduled Caste	15%
Scheduled Tribe	7.5%
Other Backward Classes (OBC)	27%
Economically Weaker Sections (EWS)	10%
Persons with Benchmark Disabilities	4%

This table shows the reservation percentage in India.

Conclusion:

In conclusion, this chapter sheds light on the critical need to reform reservation in India, unravelling its impact on students and the education landscape. It is a call to action for all stakeholders, including the judiciary, to collaboratively strive for an educational framework that truly reflects the principles of fairness, opportunity, and meritocracy.

□

Chapter XI

Violation of Human Rights Over Animal Rights

Title: "Striking a Balance: Human Rights, Animal Welfare, and Public Safety"

Introduction:

The issue of balancing human rights and animal rights is a complex and multifaceted challenge, shaped by the legal systems and societal norms in different countries. While human rights are well-established in international law, aimed at safeguarding human dignity and worth, the concept of animal rights advocates for the protection of animals from harm and exploitation. In most legal frameworks, human rights take precedence over animal rights due to the unique moral and legal status attributed to human beings. However, this chapter delves into the importance of finding a balanced approach that considers both human welfare and animal protection.

Analysis:

The chapter begins by acknowledging the established dominance of human rights in legal systems worldwide. The emphasis on human rights stems from the recognition of human beings as rational and capable of moral agency.

Consequently, human rights violations often carry severe legal penalties to uphold the dignity and well-being of individuals.

The chapter then explores the intricacies of the issue through a specific incident involving stray dogs fostered by my neighbour who bite me and my daughter while going for a morning walk For the past two years, I have been facing a distressing situation in my neighborhood. My neighbor has been fostering several dogs, which unfortunately have a history of aggressive behavior towards me and my daughter during our morning walks. These distressing encounters have instilled a deep sense of fear in our minds, leading to a significant impact on our mental and physical health.

As a result of these frightening incidents, I have been unable to maintain my regular one-hour brisk walking routine. This drastic change in my daily exercise has taken a toll on my overall health, causing me to put on a few extra kilograms of weight. The lack of physical activity and the constant fear of encountering aggressive dogs have made it difficult for me to lead a healthy lifestyle.

To address the issue, I lodged a complaint with the municipal authorities, hoping they would intervene and take necessary action. However, to my dismay, I learned that due to a PIL filed by Meneka Gandhi, dogs are not being taken to shelter homes anymore. This legal restraint has left me feeling helpless and frustrated, as the safety of the residents and their well-being should also be taken into consideration.

I earnestly hope that there will be a resolution to this distressing situation soon, and that appropriate measures will be taken to ensure the safety and peace of mind of all residents in the neighbourhood. I believe it is crucial to find a balanced approach that considers both the welfare of these dogs and the safety of the community. Until then, my daily life remains plagued by fear and the physical repercussions of the ordeal.

The incident highlights a significant challenge in implementing and enforcing laws concerning animal rights and public safety. It emphasizes the importance of striking a balance that respects both animal welfare and human safety.

Stray Dogs:

A seven-month-old baby died after being mauled by a dog. It was brutal. A woman needed 50 stitches after being bitten by her own pit bull; it also bit her two children.

Illegal dog fights are prevalent in north India and support big gambling rackets. Dogs like Rottweilers, Dobermans and Alsatians are all bred for the specific purpose of being guard dogs, or attack dogs, or police and army dogs.

The child in Noida was killed by a stray. There are an estimated 35 million stray dogs in India. This is a staggering number and a massive problem.

As many as 1.5 crore people have been bitten since 2019. Annually, 18,000 to 20,000 people die from rabies in India.

India contributes to 37 per cent of rabies deaths worldwide. It's one of the oldest zoonotic diseases, is endemic in India and has a near 100 per cent fatality rate if vaccines are not given instantly. Dogs are responsible for 97 per cent of the rabies deaths in India.

These are all unacceptable statistics, and when children are killed, it moves into the realm of the unsupportable. There is no excuse.

Where I live in the Western Cape, South Africa, I have never seen a stray dog. In my travels to many cities around the world. In cities in India, nearly every street has them.

Dogs tend to form packs, are incredibly territorial and when not in constant contact with people and gentle handling, can display high levels of aggression. There needs to be a massive movement to neuter and sterilise all strays to bring aggression levels down and check their proliferation.

More shelters are also needed. When you have dogs, especially young pups on your street, it is hard not to care for them if you are a dog lover. Khan Market in Delhi has dogs everywhere. These dogs are neutered or sterilised and fed well. They hardly bother anybody. In many other parts of the city, however, the dogs are fed but neither vaccinated, nor sterilized. Some of them can become territorial and aggressive. The feeding is often haphazard and needs to be confined to designated areas.

As pack animals, dogs will fight any other dog that is not part of the pack. The alpha is usually challenged by a rival. There are fights over mating rights. Being homeless, fighting for scraps, living within pack hierarchies makes them relatively dangerous animals to be around, especially if one does not know how to be around them.

If you are familiar with dogs and know not to show fear or try to run when faced with an aggressive dog, they will usually back away. But everyone can't be expected to either know this or learn this. People, especially children, should feel safe walking the streets.

Packs of strays in and around many of our cities have gone feral and much of the urban wildlife is either severely harmed or killed on a regular basis.

Dogs around the world have contributed to the extinction of one dozen wild bird and animal species. With our cities overflowing with garbage, which in turn attracts rats, there is continuous food supply for dogs and many stagnant water ponds, puddles and drains give them water. This allows their population to grow. If all the dogs are tagged, marked, and sterilised, their birth rates can be reduced drastically and over time, reach a stage where there are no dogs outside of shelters or home care.

It's so much better for the dogs as well, to be cared for. On the streets, many of them starve, get sick, are hit by cars, and are subjected to cruelty and tormented.

Just killing dogs is no solution. Unless our cities turn into green and clean zones overnight, we are going to have strays. Let's say a locality decides to kill the strays, dogs from other areas will move in. Nature does not permit a vacuum. The only way forward is to sterilise, vaccinate and clean your surroundings up. Timely garbage removal is key to controlling the dog population.

It's easy to target people who feed the dogs. The dogs are not around just because they are being fed, nor are they aggressive because of the feeding.

Any numbers of studies have shown that there is no predicting the aggression or why some dogs bite and some attacks are fatal. Often, the more well-fed dogs who are shown love, show less aggression.

Unfortunately, the usual reaction is that the civic staff comes by and uses horrendously cruel methods to capture the dogs. They are put to death in terrible electrocution chambers and the pain and suffering the animals face is horrific.

Children, however, are a soft target. Children between five and nine are most at risk as they flitter about outside parental supervision and are too small to be intimidating. Annually, 4.5 million children are bitten by dogs worldwide. An estimated 30 to 50 people are killed just in the US by dogs. That is 10 times more than the number killed by sharks.

To address the issue of stray animals responsibly, the chapter proposes a comprehensive approach. The suggested steps include managing stray dog populations through spaying/neutering programs, establishing animal shelters for care and adoption, educating the public about responsible pet ownership, and ensuring effective enforcement of existing laws. Cooperation between various authorities, such as the police, municipal bodies, and animal welfare organizations, is also crucial to tackle the problem collaboratively.

Conclusion:

The chapter concludes by stressing that the aim is not to prioritize animal rights over human rights but to find a compassionate and balanced approach. It underscores the significance of considering the welfare of both humans and animals in addressing such challenges. Striking a balance between human rights, animal welfare, and public safety requires a coordinated effort from authorities, fostering public awareness, and implementing effective measures to manage stray animal populations.

The incident mentioned in the chapter exemplifies the need for improvement in addressing such issues with empathy and understanding. The communication and coordination between authorities need to be enhanced to ensure public safety while responsibly handling the issue of stray animals.

Ultimately, the goal is to create a society that upholds

human rights while respecting the welfare of animals, recognizing that a compassionate approach benefits both humans and animals alike. By cultivating a harmonious coexistence between humans and animals, societies can progress towards a more ethical and compassionate future.

□

Chapter XII

A Whistleblower's Call for Justice

Title: Combating Corruption and Ensuring Accountability: Strengthening India's Governance System

In the vast landscape of India's government schemes and tenders, the battle against corruption and prolonged justice have become an urgent need. This chapter sheds light on the critical issue of state-appointed project implementation agencies being plagued by corruption, leading to severe consequences for both the projects and the people involved.

The story begins with the narrator's firsthand experience, a dedicated implementation agency working under the Ministry of Rural Development (MORD), whose noble efforts to execute a government scheme are thwarted by the influence of corrupt state officials. The state government, driven by bribery, is allocating projects to those who offer kickbacks, leaving ethical and deserving agencies in the dark.

As the chapter unravels, the focus shifts to the senior-most authority of the state government, who abuses her dominant position to suppress honest agencies and withhold funds, solely due to their refusal to engage in bribery. Such a distressing situation has forced individuals to contemplate drastic measures, with reports of people attempting suicide in despair.

I personally emphasize the dire need for a law that holds state governments accountable to the central government, ensuring that they cannot escape their responsibilities and act with impunity. To address this, a well-structured whistleblower system is proposed, giving brave individuals the power to expose corruption and intentional delays. By providing stringent powers to the central government, this mechanism would enable thorough questioning and evaluation of the state's actions, ultimately promoting transparency and accountability.

Corruption rate and steps taken:

- One common source for corruption rankings is Transparency International's Corruption Perceptions Index (CPI), which ranks countries based on perceived levels of public sector corruption. The index ranges from 0 (highly corrupt) to 100 (very clean).
- As of the last available data in 2021, India's CPI score was 40 out of 100, which placed it in the 86th position out of 180 countries surveyed. This indicates that corruption remains a significant challenge in India, but it's important to note that corruption levels can change over time.
- India scored 40 points out of 100 on the 2020 corruption perceptions index, a decrease of one point when compared with the previous year (2019). Between 2010-2020, the corruption perception index of India increased by seven points.
- Within the corruption perception index of 2020, India performs below average when compared to

other countries. India's index score has increased from a low of 33 in 2010 to a high of 40 in 2020.

- The causes of corruption in India include excessive regulations, complicated tax and licensing systems, monopoly of government-controlled institutions on certain goods and services delivery, and the lack of transparent laws and processes. According to Transparency International research, more than 62% of Indians paid bribes to public officials at some point or another.
- Denmark, New Zealand, Finland, Singapore, Sweden, and Switzerland are among the major countries with the lowest levels of corruption worldwide. Denmark and New Zealand had the highest score of 88 out of 100, followed by Finland, Switzerland, Singapore, and Sweden with a score of 85 in 2020. Countries with the highest levels of corruption worldwide include Somalia and South Sudan with a score of 12 out of 100 in 2020.
- The "Corruption Perceptions Index" for the public sector showed 60 points in India for 2022. The scale has a range from 0 to 100. The more corruption rises, the higher the number is. With this result India ranks 86th. So, compared to other countries, it is slightly below average.
- Compared to the previous year, in 2022, the level of corruption remained unchanged. In the long term, it has declined moderately in recent years.
- The United States are in 24th place with a score of 31. The ranking is led by Denmark, with a value of 10. The sad last place is occupied by Somalia (88 points).

- The causes of corruption lie in part in political and cultural reasons. Ineffective law enforcement may further promote it. It is striking that it is regularly lower in democratically governed countries (form of government in India: Federal parliamentary republic). Similarly, higher corruption occurs predominantly in low-income countries. In India, per capita income is 2,380 USD annually, which is extremely low by global standards. The cost of living is well below the global average, indicating massive socioeconomic problems.

Government of India has taken various steps and implemented measures to control corruption in the country. It's important to note that the efforts to combat corruption are ongoing, and new initiatives may have been introduced since then. Here are some of the key steps taken by the Indian government to control corruption:

- **The Lokpal and Lokayuktas Act:** The government passed the Lokpal and Lokayuktas Act in 2013, which established the Lokpal at the central level and Lokayuktas at the state level as anti-corruption ombudsman institutions. These institutions are responsible for investigating and prosecuting cases of corruption involving public servants, including politicians and government officials.
- **Whistleblower Protection:** The government enacted the Whistleblower Protection Act in 2014 to provide protection to whistleblowers who report corruption and wrongdoing. This act aims to encourage individuals to come forward with information on corruption and ensures

their safety from victimization.

- **E-Governance Initiatives:** The government has been promoting e-governance and digitalization of services to reduce opportunities for corruption and increase transparency in various administrative processes.
- **Jan Dhan Yojana:** The Pradhan Mantri Jan Dhan Yojana (PMJDY) was launched to ensure financial inclusion for all citizens. This initiative aimed to bring unbanked individuals into the formal banking system, reducing the scope for corruption in public welfare schemes.
- **Direct Benefit Transfer (DBT):** The government introduced the DBT scheme, which transfers subsidies and welfare payments directly to the beneficiaries' bank accounts. This reduces leakages and diversion of funds, minimizing corruption in social welfare programs.
- **Goods and Services Tax (GST):** The implementation of the GST in 2017 aimed to simplify the tax system and curb tax evasion, reducing corruption in the taxation process.
- **Digitization of Land Records:** Several states have undertaken initiatives to digitize land records, reducing corruption in land-related transactions and ensuring more transparent property rights.
- **Black Money Act:** The Black Money (Undisclosed Foreign Income and Assets) and Imposition of Tax Act, 2015, was enacted to tackle black money and unaccounted wealth held abroad.
- **Online Grievance Redressal Mechanisms:** The government has established online grievance

redressal mechanisms to address citizens' complaints and concerns efficiently, reducing the need for intermediaries and potential corruption.

- **Improving Transparency and Accountability:** The government has taken steps to enhance transparency and accountability in the functioning of public institutions, including introducing Right to Information (RTI) Act and various other transparency initiatives.

Additionally, public awareness, engagement, and cooperation are crucial in ensuring the success of anti-corruption efforts.

Beyond tackling corruption, the chapter underscores the importance of time-bound procedures for releasing payments. Presently, delayed funds cripple projects and inhibit progress, resulting in subpar infrastructure that deteriorates quickly under the slightest environmental pressures.

While acknowledging the existence of the court of law, the chapter stresses the necessity of a comprehensive system that ensures justice without compromising the functioning of agencies. This calls for innovative legislative amendments, empowering the judiciary to question the central government's role in monitoring state activities. By encouraging regular quality checks, India can ensure that projects meet high standards, mitigating the rapid wear and tear of public infrastructure.

Conclusion:

In conclusion, this chapter advocates for a holistic approach in combating corruption and ensuring accountability in India's governance system. By establishing a robust whistleblower mechanism, enforcing time-bound payment procedures, and encouraging judicial inquiries into the central government's oversight role, the nation can pave the way for a brighter future, characterized by transparency, efficiency, and equitable progress.

□

Chapter XIII

Overwhelmed Judiciary: A Nation's Battle with Crime and Delayed Justice

Title: "Balancing Severity and Prolonged Justice: The Struggle for Swift Resolutions in India's Judicial System"

In a nation as vast and populous as India, with its staggering 1.42 billion inhabitants, the burden of crime is an ever-present reality. Each second witnesses a new transgression, leaving no corner of the country untouched. However, amidst this relentless wave of criminality, one disturbing factor remains: the delay in providing justice to the victims.

When crimes are proven, the victims' hope for swift redressal is often dashed by the ponderous pace of the judicial process. Overloaded with an avalanche of pending cases, the Indian judiciary grapples with the mammoth challenge of delivering timely verdicts. This backlog of cases is a significant impediment, hindering the rightful resolution of heinous crimes.

"Justice delayed is justice denied" is a legal maxim meaning that if a legal remedy is available for a party that has suffered some injury, but is not forthcoming promptly, it is effectively the same as having no remedy at all. This principle is the basis for the right to a speedy trial and similar rights which are meant to expedite the legal system because it is unfair for the victim to have to sustain the injury with little hope for resolution. The phrase has become a slogan for legal reformers who view courts or governments as acting too slowly in resolving legal issues either because the existing system is too complex or overburdened, or because the issue or party in question lacks political favour.

India has an independent judicial system. Indian judicial system has a federal structure.

- Supreme Court: The Supreme Court of India is also known as the apex court of the land. It comprises 33+1 judges (33 judges + Chief justice of India). The Chief justice of India doesn't have any veto powers. He is also called "master of roaster". The Supreme Court is the top authority of law and the last appellate court in India.
- High Court: The Supreme Court is followed by the High Court as the top judicial authority of the state, controlled and headed by the chief justice of states. There are 24 high courts in India (as of 4 April, 2020).
- District Court: Last in the hierarchy is District Court also known as Subordinate Courts. These courts are controlled and managed by district and session judges under the full supervision and direction of respective high courts. The subordinate courts are further divided into 2 courts—
  - (i) Sessions Court
  - (ii) Civil Courts.

The Supreme Court and High Courts are provided with appellate jurisdiction. Appeals from the District Court go to the high court and from the High Court to the Supreme Court.

Hidden factors that slow our courts and delay justice:

Corruption in Indian Judiciary:

Is the Indian judicial system unethical? The corrupt judicial system may be one of the reasons for the delay of justice. The corrupt judges may deliberately don't announce their judgment or grant unfair adjournments to the party they favour. There may be personal bias or belief to sustain the judgment.

Indian judicial system is compared to cobweb where the small insects get caught and the big insect smashes it.

The cash at doorstep case:

Retired high court judge Nirmal Yadav was found guilty to have received Rs. 15 lakh from Delhi businessman Ravinder Singh in 2008. This money was first mistakenly delivered at the Chandigarh residence of Justice Nirmal Yadav (then a judge of Punjab and Haryana high court) on August 13, 2008. The money was alleged to have been delivered to Nirmal Yadav at her official residence the next morning. The money was taken to Justice Nirmaljit Kaur's residence by Parkash Ram, a clerk of advocate Sanjiv Bansal, then additional advocate general Haryana on directions of Ravinder Singh. When the amount reached Justice Nirmaljit Kaur's house she called Chandigarh police which seized the amount and took Parkash Ram to the police station for questioning.

Lack of Manpower:

In 2016 the then Chief Justice of India, Justice T.S. Thakur during an event started sobbing and lashed at the government "Therefore not only in the name of the litigant... the poor litigant (he pauses as his voice trembles with emotion) languishing in jail but also in the name of the country and progress, I beseech you to realise that it is not enough to criticise the judiciary...You can't shift the entire burden on the judiciary, Nothing has moved since 1987.

He referred to how the Law Commission in 1987 had recommended 40,000 judges in the country to tide over the problem of pendency of that time. Its report had said that there were only 10 judges to a million population when there should be at least 50 judges per 10 lakh population.

At the heart of the CJI's address were four strands of arguments: that judges are overwhelmed by the load of litigation; judicial vacancies are not being filled up; the appointments procedure is getting stuck at the level of the government for obscure reasons; and that without the wheels of justice turning smoothly, the common man will suffer the most.

As of 1 January, 2016, according to Court News, a publication of the Supreme Court of India, there were 16119 judges in subordinate judiciary, 598 in High Court, and 26 in Supreme Court in 2016 there were 32 million pending cases.

"It's deliberate negligence from governments that has pushed the judiciary into such a state of scarcity," says eminent jurist Ram Jethmalani. "The judiciary accounts for just 0.5 percent of the budgetary allocation."

Number Of Cases Pending:

Particulars	Civil	Criminal	Total
0 to 1 Years	963671 (22.12%)	455183 (26.65%)	1418854 (23.4%)
1 to 3 Years	667052 (15.31%)	196875 (11.53%)	863927 (14.25%)
3 to 5 Years	780927 (17.93%)	281106 (16.46%)	1062033 (17.52%)
5 to 10 Years	998176 (22.92%)	361005 (21.14%)	1359181 (22.42%)
10 to 20 Years	737572 (16.93%)	333718 (19.54%)	1071290 (17.67%)
20 to 30 Years	158232 (3.58%)	58778 (3.58%)	217010 (3.58%)
Above 30 Years	50003 (1.15%)	21201 (1.24%)	71204 (1.17%)
Total	4355633	1707866	6063499
Writ Petition	1583172	66529	1649701
Second Appeal	290102	-	290102
First Appeal	470388	395	470783
Appeal	382951	681382	1064333
Case/Petition	387449	211391	598840
Revision	86144	231873	318017
Reference	3476	576	4052
Suit	33483	-	33483
Review	21271	15	21286
Application	438948	373258	812206
Cases Instituted in Last Month	84379	64544	156169
Cases Disposed in Last Month	77747	61757	147472

Filed Cases by Senior Citizen	476504	153475	629979
Filed Cases by Woman	302733	81548	384281

This table shows the number of cases pending in India.

- In India the average pendency of any case in the 21 high courts for which we have data is about three years and one month (1,128 days). If you have a case in any of the subordinate courts in the country, the average time in which a decision is likely to be made is nearly six years (2,184 days). Even if a case does not go to the Supreme Court (and a majority of the cases in the system do not), an average litigant who appeals to at least one higher court is likely to spend more than 10 years in court. If your case does go to the Supreme Court, the average time increases by at least three more years.
- In the United States can vary significantly depending on the type of case and the court system involved. Civil and criminal cases may have different average pendency times, and they can differ between federal and state courts.

  Generally, in federal courts, civil cases may take around 18 to 24 months or more to resolve on average, while criminal cases tend to have a shorter pendency period, often taking around 12 to 18 months or less.
- In the UK can vary significantly depending on the type of case, the court's workload, and various other factors. Civil, criminal, and family cases can have different average pendency times. For

example, in the Crown Court (criminal cases), some complex cases might take several months to resolve, while simpler cases can be completed within a few weeks. In the County Courts (civil cases), the average time from filing to disposal can be several months.

Contrastingly, in some other countries, like certain Arab nations, immediate and stringent punishments for specific offenses instil deep-rooted fear in the hearts of potential wrongdoers. This fear acts as a deterrent, preventing many from venturing into criminal territory. India, too, could learn valuable lessons from these systems, contemplating the adoption of special courts or other laws designed to facilitate rapid and decisive judgments.

By empowering officials with the authority to swiftly deal with criminal matters, India could alleviate the burden on its judiciary, easing the backlog and providing a semblance of closure to countless victims. While it is essential to afford the accused a fair hearing, the present system often allocates too many opportunities for the accused to justify their actions, thus incurring significant government expenditure.

How to Improve Court Efficiency:

- By setting ADRs (Additional Dispute Resolutions) so the workload of courts can be decreased.
- By simplifying the procedure, for a speedy trial.
- By making the judicial process transparent.
- Increasing the function of Information Technology in the Judicial System.
- Improving the quality of Law Graduates.
- Advice for lawyers- Be Brief, Be Bright and Be off.
- Increasing the number of judges from lower to the top level.

- Live screening of the courts.
- Reducing the corruption in Judiciary primarily at the top level.
- Ending post-retirement jobs for the Judges.
- The appointment of upright and competent people, particularly in the higher judiciary is a sine qua non for a judiciary enjoying the confidence of the people.

J. Jayalalitha v. Union of India

The complaint against Jayalalitha that she had amassed assets beyond her known sources of income was filed in June, 1996. The first charge-sheet was filed a year later, in June 1997.

The final verdict was delivered by the Supreme Court in February, 2017 that is, twenty years after the charge sheet was filed. Jayalalitha was held guilty but by that time, as we all know, Jayalalitha had already died.

The Doshipura Graveyard Case

This is the longest trial in the history of India. It started in the year 1878 and continues till now, more than over a century compared to others. started in 1870s and though a verdict was delivered in 1981, it was never implemented. Till as recently as 2014, the two sides, Shias and Sunnis of Doshipura, were seeking further clarifications and filing fresh applications on their grievances. At the heart of the issue are nine plots in Doshipura which Shias claim as theirs, given to them by the Maharaja of Varanasi for holding religious discourses and recitations during Muharram while Sunnis claim that part of the area was their graveyard.

The disputed plots include a mosque, a baradiri and an imambara, all of which are used by both sects. There is permanent police presence in the area, which gets intensified during Muharram. Courts have ruled in favour of the Shia community with plenty of back and forth and even the state administration has been caught in the crossfire. In 1981, the Supreme Court too upheld the rights of Shias. The two graves, it was later ordered, were to be shifted with boundary walls constructed around the contested plots. In 1986, the state administration cited fear of sectarian conflict and the court put its order in abeyance for the next decade, calling for a peaceful resolution.

In 1996, the abeyance was extended by another 10 years. In 2013, the court asked Advocate General Irshad Ahmad why the dispute has been allowed to linger while in 2014, a bench comprising Justices RM Lodha, Kurian Joseph and to screen Fali Nariman declared themselves 'satisfied' that the two graves had been enclosed by a permanent masonry wall and as such 'no further order needs to be passed'. The bench did however grant the applicants liberty to make a fresh application 'narrating facts and the subsisting grievances of the applicants'

The longest trail in the US was the McMartin preschool abuse trial which continued for seven years and its cost of the investigation was $15 million and the lengthiest trial in the United Kingdom was the Jubilee line corruption trial which continued for 21 months and the cost of the trial was £60 million.

Lack of transparency:

There is a lack of transparency and accountability in the functioning of the Indian judiciary. Mysteriousness in the judicial process is a matter of public concern.

Appointment of judges:

Judges in India are appointed by a collegium as held in Three Judges Cases.

Allocation of benches:

Benches in the Supreme Court are allocated by the Chief Justice of India also known as Master of Roaster.

On 12 January, 2018 four senior-most judges of the Supreme Court held a Press conference and raised the issue of assigning cases in the apex court and flagging some other problems including issues afflicting the country's Highest Court.

Conclusion:

As a nation, India must strike a delicate balance between upholding the principles of justice and enforcing measures that prioritize the well-being of its citizens. Redefining the judicial approach and devising pragmatic solutions that expedite the legal process without compromising fairness could be the pathway to fostering a safer and more just society.

However, the road to change is fraught with challenges and demands a concerted effort from all stakeholders - lawmakers, judges, legal practitioners, and the public. Only by confronting these issues head-on and taking decisive action can India hope to overcome the burden of crime, ensure swift resolutions, and usher in a new era of justice for its people.

30 million cases are pending in the law courts. By an estimate, it will take 360 years to clear the arrears.

There is an immediate need for action. The efficiency of Indian courts can be increased by putting up the necessary norms.

Judge Jerome Frank of the US court of appeal said "I am unable to conceive that in a democracy it can never be unwise to acquaint the public with the truth about the workings of any branch of government. It is wholly undemocratic to treat the public as children who are unable to accept the inescapable shortcomings of man-made institutions. The best way to bring about the elimination of those shortcomings for our judicial system which is capable of rising elimination is to have all our citizens informed as to how that system now actually functions. it is a mistake, therefore, to try to establish and maintain through ignorance, public esteem for our courts."

"For satisfactory functioning of the judiciary, see things are necessary that judges should be honest, the judgment should be given on certain settled legal principles, and there should not be a delay and in deciding cases.

It will take unanimous and cumulative efforts by all to achieve the required progress in judicial reforms. We need radical reforms and a strong-willed to truly make a difference."

□

Chapter XIV

Shadows of Governance

Title: Unveiling Shadows: The Labyrinthine Nexus of Power

In the vibrant tapestry of India's political landscape, a disconcerting thread weaves its way through the corridors of power – the presence of politicians with criminal backgrounds. This chapter delves into the unsettling reality where the gavel and the gun seem to collide.

In a striking paradox, a person with a criminal past can vie for the highest positions in the country's leadership just six months after completing their sentence. Consequently, an unsettling number of politicians bear the marks of criminal records, raising pertinent questions about the nexus between crime and politics.

A poignant example emerges in the form of a state's Chief, embroiled in a dark history of murder and entangled in the notorious TADA case. Astonishingly, despite these grave accusations, the individual continues to hold a position of power, sending ripples of unease through the nation.

Within this labyrinth of power, those in dominant positions might manipulate circumstances to have charges acquitted, casting shadows over the sanctity of the judiciary. Witnesses vanish, evidence fades, and the elusive truth seems beyond reach, leaving society grappling with a seemingly impenetrable web of deception.

This chapter advocates for a critical amendment in the law, demanding that individuals with any criminal background, especially those accused of heinous crimes, be debarred from holding prominent political positions. Additionally, even those who manage to secure acquittal based on false evidence or lack thereof must be subject to stringent monitoring for an extended period. Only through such measures can we hope to uncover the shadows of the past and illuminate the path towards a more transparent and just political system.

Crime may evade the grasp of justice, but the indelible mark it leaves on a criminal's mind endures. As we strive for a brighter future, we must not lose sight of the complexities that intertwine crime and power, and the duty we bear to safeguard the very essence of democracy. The journey towards a more ethical and accountable governance demands collective vigilance and unyielding determination.

Criminal Involvement in Indian Politics:

The revelation of data on MLAs and ministers involved in legal trials sheds light on a concerning aspect of Indian politics. According to a report by the Association for Democratic Reforms (ADR), a significant number of elected representatives have declared criminal cases against themselves, while a majority of MLAs are crorepatis (individuals with assets worth at least one crore). This chapter delves deeper into the data and explores measures taken by other countries to disallow criminal politicians, emphasizing the urgent need for reforms and accountability in Indian politics.

The Alarming Statistics:

Out of the 558 MLAs in current state assemblies, a staggering 486 (87%) are crorepatis, raising concerns about the influence of wealth in politics.

Shockingly, 239 (43%) ministers have declared criminal cases against themselves, indicating the prevalence of criminal involvement in the corridors of power.

States with Serious Criminal Cases Among Ministers:

Maharashtra tops the list with 65% (13 out of 20) ministers facing serious criminal cases, followed by Jharkhand with 64% (7 out of 11) and Telangana with 59% (10 out of 17).

Bihar has 50% (15 out of 30) ministers with serious criminal charges, while Tamil Nadu and Punjab have 48% (16 out of 33) and 47% (7 out of 15) respectively.

Underrepresentation of Women:

Shockingly, only 9% (51 out of 558) of ministers in state assemblies are women, highlighting the glaring gender disparity in political representation.

Some states, including Arunachal Pradesh, Delhi, Mizoram, Nagaland, Meghalaya, Goa, Himachal Pradesh, Maharashtra, and Sikkim, have no women ministers, signalling a need for greater gender inclusivity in politics.

Measures Taken by Other Countries:

Several countries have implemented measures to disqualify criminal politicians from holding public office:

India: The Representation of the People Act, 1951, disqualifies individuals convicted of certain crimes from contesting elections to Parliament and State Legislatures for a specified period based on the nature of the offense.

Germany: Individuals convicted of specific crimes, especially those related to electoral integrity, can be disqualified from public office.

United States: Various state laws disenfranchise or disqualify individuals convicted of certain felonies from holding public office, with federal laws also imposing disqualifications for some crimes.

United Kingdom: The Representation of the People Act 1981 disqualifies individuals convicted of certain offenses from standing for election to the UK Parliament.

Australia: Federal and state laws disqualify individuals with criminal convictions from holding public office.

Canada: Individuals convicted of certain offenses can be disqualified from running for public office.

Urgent Need for Reforms and Accountability in India:

The prevalence of criminal involvement in politics demands urgent reforms to uphold the sanctity of the political system:

Stricter Disqualification Laws: Enhancing disqualification laws to bar individuals with serious criminal charges from contesting elections is essential for preserving the integrity of the political landscape.

Expedited Trials: Implementing fast-track trials for elected representatives accused of criminal offenses can ensure swift justice and accountability.

Transparent Candidate Selection: Political parties must adopt transparent processes for candidate selection, prioritizing ethical leadership and accountability.

Public Awareness Campaigns: Public awareness campaigns can educate voters about the criminal backgrounds of candidates, empowering citizens to make informed choices during elections.

Gender Inclusivity: Promoting greater representation

of women in politics can foster a more balanced and diverse political environment.

Conclusion:

The data on criminal involvement in Indian politics serves as a wake-up call for urgent reforms and enhanced accountability. Stricter disqualification laws, expedited trials, transparent candidate selection, public awareness campaigns, and greater gender inclusivity are imperative for preserving the sanctity of the political system. With collective efforts from political leaders, civil society, and citizens, India can pave the way for a cleaner, more accountable, and representative democracy, where criminal elements have no place in governance.

□

Chapter XV

Strengthening Mandatory provisions under Companies Act.

Title: Rectifying Loopholes in the Companies Act: Strengthening Mandatory Provisions for Effective Corporate Governance

Introduction:

Corporate Governance is the new golden term coined in the corporate sector in the late 1990's by the Industry Association On Confederation of Indian Institute which was the first initiative in India as a voluntary measure to be adopted by Indian companies. It has outlined a series of voluntary recommendations to integrate best-in-class practices of corporate governance in listed companies which touches the four cornerstones of fairness, transparency, accountability and responsibility in managing the affairs of the company. The second major initiative was taken by Security Exchange of India (SEBI) as Clause 49 of the Listing Agreement. The third key initiative to effectively introduce Corporate Governance was taken by Naresh Chandra Committee and Narayana Murthy Committee who previewed Corporate Governance model working in companies from the viewpoint of shareholders, investors and other stakeholders of the company. Corporate governance guidelines both mandated and voluntary have evolved since 1998, due to the sincere efforts of several committees appointed by the Ministry of Corporate Affairs (MCA) and the SEBI. The real change in the corporate sector could be felt with the introduction of 2009 Mandatory Corporate Governance Voluntary Guidelines which has to be comply by companies listed on stock exchange by Clause 49 of Listing Agreement including mandatory codes to be followed by companies pertaining to board of directors, audit committees and various disclosures with respect to related party transactions, whistleblower policies etc. The final assent to Corporate Governance practices in the effective management of the company can be seen as introduction to new significant provisions introduced in the Companies Act, 2013 in form of independent directors, women directors on the board, corporate social responsibility and mandatory compliance of Secretarial Standards issued by Institute of Company Secretaries of India as per Section 118 of Companies Act, 2013.

The existing loopholes in the Companies Act that allow organizations to exploit provisions, particularly regarding the appointment of a company secretary. We will highlight the importance of company secretaries in ensuring effective corporate governance and examine the consequences of non-compliance. The chapter aims to propose a stringent law to rectify these issues and create a more robust regulatory framework.

Analysis of the Existing Provisions:

We will conduct a comprehensive analysis of the Companies Act, focusing on the provision for appointing a company secretary. We will identify the specific loopholes that allow organizations to circumvent the mandatory nature of this requirement. This analysis will shed light on how these gaps in the law enable companies to exploit the provision for their benefit and may compromise corporate governance.

Need of Corporate governance:

The collapse of international giants like Eronf, Worlcom, Tyco, AOL and financial scams like Satyam have been big eye-openers in the corporate arena to make realise the company's management, ownership and stakeholders the emergent need to comply with Corporate Governance principles in order to prevent themselves from paying huge corporate criminal liabilities in the future. These huge corporate giants paid the cost for lack of good corporate governance practices and corrupt policies adopted by management of these companies and their financial consulting firms

The significance of good corporate governance solutions has widened because of the increasing conflict between ownership and management disciplines, the non-compliance of financial reporting by auditors which inflicts heavy losses on investors and lack of fair and transparent culture in the company which shook's investor trust in the financial viability of the company and its ethical standards.

Good corporate governance is embedded to the very existence of a sound company. It is important for the following reasons:

Corporate governance lays down the foundation of a properly structured Board and strives to a healthy balance between management and ownership which is capable of taking independent decisions for creating long-term trust between the company and external stakeholders of the company.

It strengthens strategic thinking at the top management by taking independent directors on the board who bring intellectual experience to the company and unbiased approach to deal with matters related to companies welfare.

It instils transparent and fair practices in the board management which results in financial transparency and integrity of the audit reports.

It sets the benchmark for the company's management to comply with laws in true letter and spirit while adhering to ethical standards of the company for bringing out effective management solutions in order to discharge its responsibility for smooth functioning of the company.

It instils loyalty among investors as their interest is looked after in the best manner by a company who adopts good management practices.

Key market players involved in corporate governance:

The Corporate management decisions have an impact on various people and entities associated with the company who are collectively known as stakeholders which include shareholders, directors, creditors, employees, suppliers, government agencies and society at large. But there are only key stakeholders like shareholders, directors, officers who are active participants in corporate governance process and other stakeholders who themselves are not involved in corporate governance practices but rather are recipients of benefits derived from companies having good corporate governance practices.

Core Principles of Corporate Governance

Transparency:

The stakeholders should be informed about the company's activities, financial statements, and the organization's performance and also at the same time it is very important to give accurate and precise information to the shareholders. Poor transparency reduces the ability to raise more capital as the investors will be unaware of vital information. It also leads to less trust among the investors as a company that is financially stable and doing well will not have anything to hide. Moreover, companies that are doing well will like to make the financial statements public to promote themselves. Transparency in financial reporting increases the confidence of the shareholders will help them. The policies must be formulated in a manner which ensures transparency.

Transparency should also be maintained between directors and employees. The directors should be easily accessible by the employees and directors should be open to ideas of the management and employees. This makes employees more committed to the vision of the company. Lack of transparency will always lead to confusion and it will hinder the productivity of the management and employees.

Accountability:

To achieve the goals and objectives of the company, people should be held accountable at all levels. Employees should be accountable to the management, management should be accountable to the board of directors and the board of directors should be accountable to investors and shareholders. Employees, management staff and directors will learn from the mistakes if they are made accountable and it leads to better utilization of the available resources. In this way the organization will grow faster as the scope for mistakes will reduced considerably. It is the duty of directors to encourage accountability in the organization.

Responsibility:

The directors of the company are primarily responsible to the shareholders, employees and the whole society. The directors of the company should work in the best interests of the company and its employees. It is the duty of the directors to determine the responsibility of the management and employees. Also, management and employees should be held accountable to make sure that responsibilities are carried out properly. Shareholders want directors to be responsible to their needs and maximize the value of the firm.

Fairness:

Fairness principle not only enhances corporate value but it also leads to efficiency in resource allocation. All shareholders and investors should receive equal treatment by the company and the directors should try to prevent conflict of interests. It is very important to ensure fairness in transactions which are entered by the company. For e.g. a company should not enter into related party transactions without getting the approval of the shareholder. Effective communication mechanisms should be adopted by the company to make sure policies and financial statements are informed to the shareholders.

Shareholder Engagement:

Shareholders should not be kept in the dark and must be informed of the financial position and organizational objectives. Minority and majority shareholders should be treated equally. All transactions must be avoided which might lead to conflicts with the shareholders.

Leadership:

Board of directors is the brain of any company and it

is under their leadership and guidance that any company expands and prospers. The directors should be committed to fulfilling the vision and mission of the company which is mentioned the constitution documents. Leadership also includes motivating the employees so that they reach the maximum potential. It also includes effective decision making and capitalize on opportunities to benefit the firm. Poor leadership by the board can create problems for the company and which may eventually end in bankruptcy or shutting down.

Key features of corporate governance in Companies Act, 2013:

There has been a sea change in companies Act, 2013 which has waved its way from principle of corporate governance practices as the new key change in the act. The Companies Act, 2013 has taken a foot forward from SEBI's Clause 49 of listing agreement by introducing provisions in the companies act 2013 which promotes corporate governorship code in such a manner that it will no longer be restricted to only listed public companies but also unlisted public companies. Companies Act, 2013 lays greater emphasis on corporate governance as it clearly provides the rules and regulations for the same.

Why do Companies need good Corporate Governance?

Every company should have an ethical corporate governance code as it reduces the risk of fraudulent activities by the top management. Good corporate governance structure enables accountability in the organization and also makes sure that directors, management and employees do not indulge in fraudulent and unlawful activities. The company is responsible for the welfare of the shareholders, management and employees and it is very important to protect their rights. A transparent and ethical corporate governance structure will enhance investor's trust. It will also have an internal control framework which helps in mitigating future risks. Poor corporate governance can always lead to conflict among the shareholders which can always tarnish a company's image. Tarnished image of the company may also lead to dissatisfied and frustrated employees.

Companies Act, 2013 gives a lot of importance to ethical corporate structure by penalizing the officer in default if they do not comply with the same. A director or a KMP can be held liable for unlawful or illegal activities committed by him. It is the duty of the board of directors to have a good corporate governance practice in its company. Independent directors also play a vital role in having effective corporate governance by helping the company formulate policies and representing the shareholders' grievances.

Corporate governance practices in India:

The organizational framework for corporate governance initiatives in India consists of the Ministry of Corporate Affairs (MCA) and the Securities and Exchange Board of India (SEBI). SEBI monitors and regulates corporate governance of listed companies in India through Clause 49. This clause is incorporated in the listing agreement of stock exchanges with companies and it is compulsory for listed companies to comply with its provisions. MCA through its various appointed committees and forums such as National Foundation for Corporate Governance (NFCG), a not-for-profit trust, facilitates exchange of experiences and ideas amongst corporate leaders, policy makers, regulators, law enforcing agencies and non- government organizations.

The Importance of Company Secretaries in Corporate Governance:

We have delved into the crucial role that company secretaries play in ensuring effective corporate governance. We will discuss how these professionals act as a link between the board of directors, management, shareholders, and other stakeholders. Additionally, we will highlight their responsibilities in maintaining compliance, ethical standards, and legal obligations. This chapter will underscore the significance of a company secretary's presence in fostering transparent and responsible corporate practices.

This pivotal chapter will propose a new stringent law to rectify the identified loopholes and make the appointment of a company secretary mandatory for all organizations, regardless of size or ownership structure. We will explore the potential changes needed in the Companies Act and suggest additional measures to reinforce the compliance of this provision. The aim is to create a more robust legal framework that ensures corporate accountability and transparency.

The concept of the escalation clause in laws. While it serves as an essential mechanism to accommodate exceptional circumstances, we will highlight its potential shortcomings and limitations. Understanding these limitations will help us strike a balance between flexibility and firmness in enforcing mandatory provisions. Delicate balance required between flexibility and strictness in laws. We will analyse various scenarios and consider the consequences of imposing stringent regulations on certain provisions while allowing leeway in others. Striking the right balance is crucial to fostering a business environment that encourages growth and innovation while safeguarding against malpractices.

Landmark Cases

Salomon v Salomon & Co. Ltd:

Details of the Case:

In 1892, Aaron Salomon incorporated his business, designating himself as the sole shareholder along with his wife, daughter, and four sons.

The managing director of the business, Mr. Salomon, sold it for 39,000 and removed a $10,000 debt.

Edmund Broderip gave Mr. Salomon an advance of $5,000 in exchange for the debentures' security.

Sales soon began to decline, and this was followed by strikes, which in turn caused a downturn in business.

In order to enforce security, Mr. Edmund sued Mr. Salomon due to his position and duty within the company.

Verdict:

As a result of the company's legal separation from its members, Mr. Salomon, the founder, is shielded in this instance from personal liability to creditors.

The court maintained the idea of corporate personhood as defined by the Companies Act of 1862.

For this reason, creditors of a bankrupt company cannot take the company's shareholders to court to collect unpaid debts.

Seth Mohan Lal v. Grain Chambers Ltd:

Details of the Case:

The respondent corporation was founded with the intention of carrying out particular activities related to the trading of commodities, including jaggery.

All members of the company are required by the AOA to participate in the business transactions of the company.

The 1913 Companies Act, which did not impose any

restrictions on a director's ability to transact with the corporation, was applied to these transactions.

The Act was amended in 1936 to forbid directors from doing business with the corporation.

The Company's business plan, however, didn't alter. The respondent and the appellant company had engaged in a transaction, with the appellant company making sizeable financial deposits into the respondent's account as part of the transaction.

The respondent and the appellant company had engaged in a transaction, with the appellant company making sizeable financial deposits into the respondent's account as part of the transaction.

The Indian government issued an order on February 15, 1950, that made it illegal for anyone to make or receive payments related to any futures after that date, or to participate in "future" jaggery transactions.

following such resolution by submitting a petition against the corporation and shutting down operations in order to settle all outstanding debts before the closing date at the going rate.

Verdict:

The notification nullifies any pending guts and futures transactions, the appeals court decided.

Because of this, the company's closure was not supported by any evidence, and the warning against futures trading in the gut was intended to be effective.

Conclusion:

The Companies Act, 2013 empowers independent directors with proper checks and balances so that such extensive powers are not exercised in an unauthorized manner but in a rational and accountable way. The changes are a step forward in the right direction to smoothly run the management and affairs of the companies in the interest of stakeholders. These are all welcome changes in the globalised corporate world of today and they will strengthen the core corporate machinery by instilling strong corporate governance norms in a company leading to economic efficiency and higher ethical standards which will always inspire the company's management to work in the direction to uphold its goals of maximization of wealth of stakeholders backed with good corporate repute.

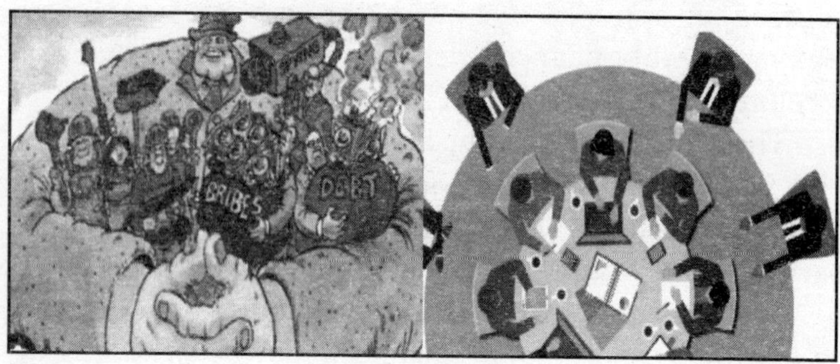

□

Reference

https://www.oecd.org/daf/ca/corporategovernanceprinciples/43654301.pdf

https://www.worlddata.info/average-age.php

https://en.wikipedia.org/w/index.php?title=Retirement_age&action=edit§ion=6

http://www.mca.gov.in/SearchableActs/Section135.htm

http://www.mca.gov.in/Ministry/pdf/CompaniesActNotification22014.pdf

Governance 101 All you need to know on corporate governance practices in India (deloitte.com)

https://blog.oureducation.in/political-scenario-in-india/

https://www.ojjdp.gov/ojstatbb/crime/qa05101.asp

https://www.ojjdp.gov/ojstatbb/crime/qa05101.asp?qaDate=2020

https://en.wikipedia.org/wiki/Rape_statistics

https://www.jagranjosh.com/general-knowledge/list-of-all-the-political-parties-in-india-1476786411-1

https://www.investopedia.com/insights/worlds-top-economies/

Minimum Educational Qualifications Required for Politicians in India (ipleaders.in)

The Benefits of Legal Insurance: Peace of Mind and Financial Protection (linkedin.com)

What is Legal Insurance and Is it Worth It? | MetLife

Rethinking Reservation Policies in India (drishtiias.com)

Trial by Fire: The Tragic Tale of the Uphaar Fire Tragedy Book by Shekhar Krishnamoorthy

Anita Gets Bail: What Are Our Courts Doing? What Should We Do About Them? Book by Arun Shourie

https://services.ecourts.gov.in/ecourtindia_v6/static/about-us.php

Whither Indian Judiciary Book by J. Markandey Katju

https://m.timesofindia.com/city/chandigarh/cash-at-doorstep-r-k-jains-statement-recorded/amp_articleshow/57381129.cms

https://www.deccanherald.com/india/uttar-pradesh-woman-entrepreneur-dies-after-traffic-stopped-for-presidents-visit-1001804.html

https://indianexpress.com/article/india/president-ram-nath-kovind-kanpur-blockade-covid-patient-7377557/

https://www.thehindu.com/news/national/CJI-Thakur%E2%80%99s-emotional-appeal-to-Modi-to-protect-judiciary/article14257126.ece

https://testbook.com/ias-preparation/reservation

https://www.legalserviceindia.com/legal/article-8705-famous-cases-under-company-law.html

"Justice delayed is justice denied" - how can we deal with the inefficiency of courts in a fast-changing society - iPleaders

https://www.google.com/search?sca_esv=600662400&rlz=-
1C1ONGR_enIN1056IN1058&sxsrf=ACQVn0_U7XlOx-
4lOX0VxiQS3kO92WDZ5Vg:1705993818035&q=explor-
ing+age+and+work+in+challengin+world&tbm=isch&-
source=lnms&sa=X&ved=2ahUKEwjj7IycvKDAxUwT2wGHfnw-
CDAQ0pQJegQIDRAB&biw=1366&bih=607&dpr=1#imgrc=aHL-
r6vQoB8RxdM

https://www.google.com/search?sca_esv=600662400&rlz=-
1C1ONGR_enIN1056IN1058&sxsrf=ACQVn0ZyV1FjPmqOSQ-
5yk92IyHTuRrUoQ:1705993539478&q=after+retirement&t-
bm=isch&source=lnm&sa=X&ved=2ahUKEwiFmaOXfKDAx-
WhxDgGHQuCBtIQ0pQJegQIChAB&biw=1366&bih=607&d-
pr=1#imgrc=x-wkCTYF8owmbM

https://www.google.com/search?q=without+life+insurance&tb-
m=isch&ved=2ahUKEwid0ZmF8fKDAxWNQWwGHVJ0B88Q2c-
CegQIABAA&oq=without+life+insurance&gs_lcp=CgNpbW-
cQAzIFCAAQgAQyBggAEAUQHjIGCAAQCBAeMgYIABAIEB-
46BAgjECc6BggAEAcQHjoHCAAQgAQQGDoICAAQBRAHEB-

46CAgAEAgQBxAeUMsaWMglYN86aABwAHgAgAGbAYgBsAaSAQMwLjaYAQCgAQGqAQtnd3Mtd2l6LWltZ8ABAQ&sclient=img&ei=ulyvZZ2MBY2DseMP0uidAw&bih=607&biw=1366&rlz=1C1ONGR_enIN1056IN1058#imgrc=54fx1xFQ15HRkM

https://www.google.com/search?sca_esv=601011473&rlz=1C1ONGR_enIN1056IN1058&sxsrf=ACQVn06nvmicDISkB5WS44HbmNVRYA9A:1706081406409&q=life+insurance&letbm=isch&source=lnms&sa=X&ved=2ahUKEwi9hr_BwPWDAxVDTgGHR3TArYQ0pQJegQIDhAB&biw=1366&bih=607&dpr=1#imgrc=-Q92Fl0Kqol5mM

https://www.google.com/search?q=sex+work+is+work&tbm=isch&ved=2ahUKEwiUs_G1xOuDAxW7SmcHHWv6BlcQ2cCegQIABAA&oq=sex+w&gs_lcp=CgNpbWcQARgAMgQIIxAnMgUIABCABDIFCAAQgAQyBQgAEIAEMgUIABCABDoGCAAQCBAeOgkIABAIEB4QxwM6CQgAEAcQHhDHAzoGCAAQBxAeOggIABAIEAcQHjoICAAQgAQQsQM6BAgAEANQpAZY9h5gqixoAHAAeACAAaQBiAGDCZIBAzAuOZgBAKABAaoBC2d3cy13aXotaW1nwAEB&sclient=img&ei=aoKrZZTWGbuVnesP6_SbuAU&bih=607&biw=1366&rlz=1C1ONGR_enIN1056IN1058#imgrc=o0b9Fn9W9BbUEM

https://www.google.com/search?q=happy+women+day&tbm=isch&ved=2ahUKEwjU77vbwfWDAxWZ2wGHQdCBtMQ2cCegQIABAA&oq=happy+women+day&gs_lcp=CgNpbWcQAzIECCMQJzIECAAQHjIECAAQHjIECAAQHjIECAAQHjIECAAQHjIECAAQHjIECAAQHjIECAAQHjIECAAQHjoFCAAQgAQ6CggAEIAEEIoFEENQxwZYnRBg6hdoAHAAeACAAZcBiAG0BZIBAzAuNZgBAKABAaoBC2d3cy13aXotaW1nwAEB&sclient=img&ei=wb2wZZSLE77PseMPh4SZmA0&bih=607&biw=1366&rlz=1C1ONGR_enIN1056IN1058#imgrc=MjeMk_AcwAiPsM

https://www.google.com/search?sca_esv=601011473&rlz=1C1ONGR_enIN1056IN1058&sxsrf=ACQVn08qwk55ByT6mORXg7bMqKRH7JR6TQ:1706081918566&q=commercial+disputes&tbm=isch&source=lnms&sa=X&sqi=2&ved=2ahUKEwiOwtq1wvWDAxWQ3jgGHXvBAawQ0pQJegQIDBAB&biw=1366&bih=607&dpr=1#imgrc=sX0IdOnDvH_ttM

https://www.google.com/search?sca_esv=601011473&rlz=1C1ONGR_enIN1056IN1058&sxsrf=ACQVn08qwk55ByT6mORXg7bMqKRH7JR6TQ:1706081918566&q=commer-

cial+disputes&tbm=isch&source=lnms&sa=X&sqi=2&ved=2ahUKEwiOwtq1wvWDAxWQ3jgGHXvBAawQ0pQJegQIDBAB&biw=1366&bih=607&dpr=1#imgrc=VPemiDelqvhuIM

https://www.google.com/search?q=delay+justice&tbm=isch&ved=2ahUKEwi30N76w_WDAxVKTmwGHW6TDOsQ2cCegQIABAA&oq=delay+justice&gs_lcp=CgNpbWcQAzIFCAAQgAQyBQgAEIAEMgYIABAHEB4yBggAEAcQHjIGCAAQBxAeMgYIABAHEB46BAgjECc6BggAEAgQHjoNCAAQgAQQigUQQxCxAzoKCAAQgAQQigUQQzoICAAQgAQQsQNQqAZYrypglD5oAXAAeACAAZUBiAGhC5IBBDAuMTGYAQCgAQGqAQtnd3Mtd2l6LWltZ8ABAQ&sclient=img&ei=G8CwZffWLsqcseMP7qay2A4&bih=607&biw=1366&rlz=1C1ONGR_enIN1056IN1058#imgrc=_YT7r-5JCi_jTM

https://www.google.com/search?sca_esv=600017421&rlz=1C1ONGR_enIN1056IN1058&sxsrf=ACQVn08zmTiJHRUS46h_2cTE8XwiXb1IyA:1705735265659&q=fast+track+court&tbm=isch&source=lnms&sa=X&ved=2ahUKEwjFqdyEtuDAxUG2DgGHeUBU8Q0pQJegQICxAB&biw=1366&bih=607&dpr=1#imgrc=e8ogv4OxXtWHEM

https://www.google.com/search?sca_esv=601011473&rlz=1C1ONGR_enIN1056IN1058&sxsrf=ACQVn08EM9cDoQ2r2XZzUhEtPmyz9eUykA:1706082965108&q=reservation&tbm=isch&source=lnms&sa=X&ved=2ahUKEwimvN6oxvWDAxVy1jgGHUUQAxQQ0pQJegQICxAB&biw=1366&bih=607&dpr=1#imgrc=o8QCensjwDUbqM

https://www.google.com/search?sca_esv=601011473&rlz=1C1ONGR_enIN1056IN1058&sxsrf=ACQVn0M5hbiwLV7tNyMcvyikcgTUo26A:1706082924817&q=reforming+reservation&tbm=isch&source=lnms&sa=X&ved=2ahUKEwjXqMOVxvWDAxXOyqACHeOXDDUQ0pQJegQIDBAB&biw=1366&bih=607&dpr=1#imgrc=dRiL1ZUUlhD8yM

https://learn.finology.in/courses/legal/code-of-civil-procedure

https://indianexpress.com/

https://njdg.ecourts.gov.in/njdgnew/index.php